ELEVATOR
BABIES

Andrew Puckey

ARCHWAY
PUBLISHING

Archway Publishing books may be ordered
through booksellers or by contacting:

Archway Publishing
1663 Liberty Drive
Bloomington, IN 47403
www.archwaypublishing.com
1 (888) 242-5904

Because of the dynamic nature of the Internet, any web addresses or
links contained in this book may have changed since publication and
may no longer be valid. The views expressed in this work are solely those
of the author and do not necessarily reflect the views of the publisher,
and the publisher hereby disclaims any responsibility for them.

Any people depicted in stock imagery provided by Thinkstock are
models, and such images are being used for illustrative purposes only.
Certain stock imagery © Thinkstock.

ISBN: 978-1-4808-4339-4 (sc)
ISBN: 978-1-4808-4340-0 (e)

Library of Congress Control Number: 2017901581

Print information available on the last page.

Archway Publishing rev. date: 02/27/2017

For Kristine, my best friend

CONTENTS

AUTHOR'S NOTE

There are a few words in these stories, while I do not condone their usage now as an adult, were commonly and widely used around the neighborhood while growing up. I have chosen to include this language in places I deemed absolutely necessary to convey the emotions of the characters. It is not meant to purposely offend others. Language is always evolving, changing. As an author, and a teacher, it is my hope that these words here on the page might be able to educate, and to show how far we have come in just a few short years.

ROCK WARS

When I was in the third grade there was no one cooler than my cousins, Matt and Mike. Not only were they cool, but they were identical twins, which raised the coolness factor even more. Plus, they were two years older than me. I was pretty sure they knew everything, so getting me to go along with their adventures was easy. Getting out of trouble once we had those adventures was not.

My cousins only lived two miles away from me, but at that age two miles was no different than Timbuktu. Our families were together a lot, but that was on the weekends. During the week we went to different schools, had different friends, and lived different lives. So when we got together on Saturday night or Sunday afternoon, it was time to share stories and catch up. Their stories always seemed better than mine even though I tried my best to match them. It was impossible. No matter what I said, they could beat it, so I always ended up just listening to them.

Not that listening to them was a bad thing. They had tons of cool things to teach me, like who was the best football or baseball player of all time or the proper technique to shoot free-throws. We built tree forts and fixed our bikes so we could race them across the park; we sailed ships in the pond and made slingshots together so we could sink them in glorious kamikaze air raids; we played stickball and freeze tag and a lot of crazy games that I didn't play with the kids in my neighborhood. The games always had some caveat attached to them, like "Walnut Street Rules" or "Cracker Jack Law," which meant nothing to me until I did something wrong and all the kids would scream at me. It's not that it was any different in my neighborhood. If a ball went under a car, it was a double. If it got stuck somewhere and you had to climb to get it down, you were out, and you did the climbing. Like any kid, I adapted quickly and took the standard abuse until I got it right.

"Hey kid, I don't know how you do it in your neighborhood, but here that's an 'Oak Street Fly Rule Single,'" someone would yell.

"Matt and Mike, why don't you teach your cousin something before you let him play?" someone else would holler.

"Why don't you shut up or I'll shut you up," Matt would say.

"Yeah, he's just learning and he's still better than you," Mike would answer.

It made me feel good when my older cousins stuck up for me, especially because they weren't afraid of the kids who were older than them. Like I said, they were cool, and there were two of them, so it was double trouble if you got into a scrap.

When summer rolled around it was even better. Since they were older, my cousins were allowed to ride their bikes farther than I ever could, which meant I got to go with them to Lengel's Market. We'd get ice cream, soda pop, and Snickers bars. It was the best. One time my uncle even took time off and took us all to Shea stadium for an afternoon Mets game. My cousins were crazy about the Amazin's. That was one thing they tortured me about because I was a Yankees fan. They made a good case for Nolan Ryan being the best pitcher ever, but they couldn't sell me off of The Bambino. That afternoon I cheered like crazy for The

Mets, who won in the bottom of the ninth, but it still didn't change my opinion about Yankee Stadium, where my dad took me to my first ballgame. It was a much better stadium, partly because I saw the Yankees beat the Red Sox, and partly because I was with my dad.

Summer was also great because we got to have sleepovers. Usually, my cousins wanted me to stay at their house. That was fun, but sometimes I wanted them to stay at my house so I could show them off to my friends. I didn't understand why they wouldn't stay over until I was at their house one night. It was bedtime and my cousin said he was thirsty, but my aunt wouldn't let him have a drink. I had never seen anything so mean before. My aunt was always so nice, but no matter how much Matt whined, she wouldn't give in.

"Matthew, you know what happens every time. Just go to sleep," she said.

"Ma, I'm not a baby. Just let me get a drink," Matt complained.

"Do you want me to get your father? Do you? Now go to sleep!" she said and closed the door.

Matt listened carefully until he heard his parent's door shut, then he crept out to the kitchen. He moved without a sound, another great trick he taught me, and was gone for what seemed like forever. The suspense was almost too much to bear, but just when I thought I had to go after him he reappeared in the doorway, grinning and holding three Cokes. We couldn't help but celebrate our victory by staying up laughing and listening to Matt's story of how he completed his mission. That was what he called it, a mission, and from then on all of us started calling anything that could get us into trouble "missions." The victory was short lived because we were shushed from down the hall by my aunt, but I went to sleep that night as proud of my cousins as I ever had been.

The morning was a different story. I awoke in a foggy stupor, groggy from not enough sleep because we had stayed up so late. But there was something else. There was an odd smell, pungent like the lion cage at the zoo. And there was something else - the bed was wet and cold. I jumped up and threw the covers on the floor. I looked in shock at the giant wet spot on the bed and then I knew. It was pee – but it wasn't mine. My pajamas were wet where I laid in it, but not in the front. My cousins had twin beds and I had slept with Matt in his bed, but he was gone. And so was Mike. I pulled back the covers on his bed and looked in horror at an identical wet spot. As the realization dawned on me, disgust overtook me. I mouthed the words, afraid to say them aloud: "They're bed wetters. Twin pissers!"

Just then Matt and Mike came back into the room, wearing different pajamas than they had on last night. From the sheepish looks on their faces I could tell they knew I knew, but they were not going to volunteer to tell me anything.

"You...you...peed the bed," I said, looking at both of them.

"What?" Matt said with genuine shock. This threw me because it was so obvious, how could he deny it?

"You. Peed. The. Bed." Each word was a gunshot, aimed squarely at Matt.

"No I didn't," he said. "You did."

My mind was thoroughly blown. He did it, but he was saying it was me. How could he do that? I had never wet the bed. Now, I'm soaked with his pee and he dared to blame me?

"I woke up this morning," Matt continued, "in a puddle of your pee. You should be thankful I'm even talking to you."

What the devil was he talking about? I was the one who was upset here.

"Matt, there is no way I peed the bed. Look, the front of my pajamas aren't even wet. And you're wearing different pajamas. And look!" I threw the blanket from Mike's bed on the floor. "Look! Did I pee his bed, too?"

This was unexpected. It was clear they had coordinated their plan, hoping to wake me up and blame me, figuring I wouldn't find Mike's bed and then clean up when I went to the bathroom. But I was one step ahead of them and they were trapped.

"You're…you're…peebags! You're bedwetting babies! You're peebags!" It was the only thing I could think to say and I just kept saying it, over and over.

Their faces were red and I could feel their shame. This was no ordinary secret. This was the deepest and darkest of all secrets and had to be kept at all costs. It could ruin a normal kid, so what would it do to the two coolest kids on the block? Things started to make a lot more sense to me now. No wonder they wouldn't stay over. Their room always smelled clean, like bleach, because their mom must wash the sheets every day. And their "mattress protectors?" Rubber sheets to keep the pee out. My world was in chaos, the kind that can only occur when your heroes fall.

"Don't tell our mom," Matt said.

"Yeah, we'll get in big trouble because she knows this happens and she's sick of doing laundry," Mike said. "She tells us everyday."

"This happens everyday?" I asked.

"Well, no," Mike said. "It hasn't happened in awhile, like two months. My mom never lets us drink anything before bed anymore."

"You won't tell our mom, will you?" Matt asked.

"Or anyone else," Mike added.

That's when the bribery started. They told me how cool I was, and how I was their favorite cousin. They promised me anything, because as it turned out, their father promised to take them to do whatever they wanted if they made it a month without an accident. They were three days away. It was too much to watch them keep begging.

"All right, guys, it's all right. I won't tell. I just need to get out of these pee clothes."

I started to change and they took the room apart. First they opened the windows – got to air it out they said. Then they stripped the sheets and made their beds, or so they looked made anyway. Then they jammed the sheets behind their dressers. The plan was to throw them in the wash when their mom started it, then tell her they'd put the clothes in the dryer, to help her out. This, of course, would not arouse suspicion because most eleven year old boys do laundry for their mother…

They had already stashed their pajamas under Mike's bed (Matt's idea) and were ready to go out and play when I came back from cleaning up. My aunt and uncle suspected nothing, but why would they? They weren't awake and when I looked at the clock I saw why: It was 5:30a.m.

To kill time we ate bowls of Cap'n Crunch in front of the T.V., keeping the sound down low so no one woke up, and then played some games until it was almost 7a.m., then we hit the street.

Matt and Mike promised me an awesome day, the best ever, and it started by riding up the street on our bikes to see if anyone else was up. They weren't, so we stopped by the house to pick up some fishing poles and then go to the river. We didn't catch anything, but it was fun and by the time we rode home everyone was out playing. We stopped by another kid's house to check out the coolest tree ever, with vines you could swing on, my cousins said. This would be the highlight of my day I was told, better than anything we'd ever done before.

Matt and Mike walked up on the porch and knocked. No one answered so they started to whisper to one another. I couldn't understand everything they were saying, but I made out a few things.

"Is he still on vacation?" Mike asked.

"Yeah, he won't be back, no one will know," Matt said as they came off the porch.

"What's up guys?" I asked.

"Nothing," they said in unison. Then Matt said, "It's fine. Our friend isn't here right now, but he said we can play here whenever we want. Let's go."

We walked around the side of the house to the small backyard and sure enough, there was a great big elm tree. The tree looked dead, like something in a horror movie. It towered over a dilapidated old tool shed that was leaning over, boards broken, nails sticking out, with vines hanging down on its roof. There was nothing safe about this situation, a mother's worst nightmare of cautionary tales waiting to be told.

"The mission, gentlemen," Matt started, "is to climb the tree, storm the shed, and swing to freedom!"

With a mighty yell we began our assault. Climbing the tree was easy, but getting to the top of the shed required a small leap, one that looked much farther away from the air than on the ground. Mike jumped first. He landed, almost on his feet, and stood up.

"Come on, you wimps! It's easy," he said.

I jumped next, lost my balance when I hit and the shed shook, then got on my feet. When Matt landed, his left foot went through the shed's roof, leaving him trapped as the shed listed slowly to the right, then stopped when Mike and I ran to the left edge.

"This things going down," Matt said, still trying to get his foot free.

"I'm outta here!" Mike said, grabbing a vine and swinging off the roof.

It was the coolest thing ever. He did look just like Tarzan, swinging off the roof and letting go just a few feet off the ground.

"Did you see that? Nothing to it," he shouted up to us.

"Go ahead," Matt told me, "you go next."

"Okay," I answered. I'll admit I was scared, but I wouldn't let my cousins know it. I grabbed a thick vine and swung out. It was something I'll never forget – being free and flying through the air. It was perfect, except I was too afraid to let go and swung back to slam into the shed. It knocked the wind out of me and caused Matt and Mike to go into a fit of laughter.

"You idiot," Mike said, "you have to let go or you'll kill yourself!"

Matt laughed less because the shed had started to move again. I let myself drop to the ground, a little more embarrassed than bruised, and joined Mike.

"I'll show you how it's done," Matt said.

He ran and jumped on the big vine, swinging far out away from the shed. But there was no give in the vine or the branch it was hanging from so Matt was really airborne. He realized he couldn't let go and we watched as he swung back towards the shed. Unlike me, he pulled his legs up and landed back on the roof with a thud. That's when the shed started to go.

The sound is difficult to describe unless you've ever heard old nails being pulled out of old wood, seasoned with time but solid and sound, reluctant to be separated from one another. It's a screeching noise that grows in intensity, rises in pitch, and usually culminates in disaster.

Matt didn't get to see it. In something out of an action movie he started to ride the shed down, then jumped at the last second to a low hanging vine, and landed, just beyond the crashing shed, on his feet. He turned just in time to watch the dust rise. It was amazing. In the future, that story would be retold many times by kids who heard it, but never, even with all the added exaggeration, could it match what really happened. And that's when Sean Mulligan came home.

"What did you do to my shed?" he asked in a stunned voice.

"Whoops," came from both twins at once.

"My father is going to kill you," Sean said. "Who told you it was even okay to come in my yard?"

Matt and Mike had neglected to mention that they didn't really know Sean. They had heard of his jungle-swing tree and shed from a kid who heard it from a kid. They had ridden by the house before, so they knew right where it was but had never actually been here. Sean was a full year older than my cousins and lived three blocks east, so it was really another world. Even so, everyone had a general idea of who was living around the area, from school or sports or word of mouth. It didn't mean that everyone was friends.

"Hey, take it easy," Mike said.

"Yeah, your shed almost killed me," Matt said.

Sean stared at them in disbelief. Matt just told him that somehow this was his fault, and since I had just experienced this same reasoning earlier this morning, I could understand his bewilderment. Finally, after a long pause where I thought we were going to leave, Sean spoke.

"You…you broke my shed. And came in my yard and trespassed on my property. You have to pay for this!"

"Hey pal," Matt started, "you should have been here to tell us. We could've been killed."

"This is not my problem," Sean said. "This is your problem and you need to fix it."

"What do you want us to do, build you a new shed? That

thing was a piece of junk!" Mike told him. "Besides, are you going to tell your mommy on us you wuss? There are three of us and we'll all say you were here and you broke the shed."

This devious reasoning was amazing to me. I never knew you could convince someone that they were wrong when they were completely right. That may be why I always thought at least one of the twins would be a lawyer, but that never happened. Sean was also amazed. He was getting angrier and angrier, and I could tell he wanted to hit someone, but he was scared because he was outnumbered.

"Look, why don't you play smart and just pretend this never happened?" Matt asked. "Just go away all day so when your parents get home you can say you didn't do it and you don't know how it happened."

"Yeah," Mike said, "it will work like a charm. That old shed was bound to fall over sometime. Then no one gets in trouble."

"Yeah," Matt jumped in, "you don't want to be a tattle-tale. You're too cool for that."

The charm was winning Sean over. It all made perfect sense. No one had to get in trouble. Everything would be all right. He was cool. He didn't tattle-tale on people.

"Well, all right," Sean said. "I won't tell…"

The words weren't out of his mouth and we were on our bikes and headed up the road.

"You're okay," Mike said. "Stay cool."

"Chump!" Matt said as we got a little further, and we laughed all the way back to their house.

Matt and Mike seemed invincible. They could do anything. Matt retold us his story and then told everyone on his block. By three o'clock that afternoon, it was becoming legend. We were still celebrating when Sean and his cronies showed up.

"Sean, what are you doing here?" Matt asked. He didn't look worried, but his voice sounded nervous.

"My dad came home," he said.

"Did you tell him what we said?" Mike asked.

"Yes, and it didn't work," Sean said. "He didn't believe me and I got it good. Now you scumbags are gonna pay for it."

"Whoa, whoa, whoa. First, who you calling scumbags?" Matt asked. "Second, what did you tell your dad? You probably screwed it up."

"I didn't tell him nothing...except when he got home I was there. So I told him I saw it fall over from the wind."

"You idiot," Matt said. "We told you not to be home and then just deny any knowledge. You got what you deserved because you were too stupid to follow the perfect plan!"

Now, Sean was pissed. His face was beat red and he started to shake. He had now been embarrassed in front of his friends, by guys who were younger than him, and this wouldn't stand.

"You...you...you lying pieces of crap! I'm gonna punch your faces in!"

Sean started for Matt but stopped when Matt and Mike came for him. I always thought of them by what adults called them, blue-eyed, blonde haired angels, but not today. They were screaming banshees. Sean screamed too, but like a scared girl, and retreated to his group of friends.

"No fair! There are two of you and one of me!"

"Well, you've got a problem with both of us," Mike said.

"And this is our turf," Matt said, "so now you have a problem with all of us!"

Sean had brought seven or eight guys with him, but they weren't enough and he knew it would be a slaughter. He didn't want to back down again. He was thinking about a tactical retreat but wasn't fast enough. He was surrounded.

"Looks like we can settle this right now or…" Matt said as the idea overtook him, "we can have a Rock War!"

There was a collective gasp from the crowd. Rock Wars were legendary. They were also bloody, painful, and ill-advised from an adult perspective, so no one had been involved in a true Rock War in forever. A few of the kids would tell stories of the last great Rock War, that their brothers had fought in, but those brothers were away at college now or just never around to verify the truthfulness. A real Rock War was something everyone dreamed of participating in before they died. The rules were pretty simple: Each group started at their end of the street and ran towards one another flinging rocks until one group ran away. It was like a movie style street gang rumble, only even more stupid than anyone could ever imagine. However, at this age, it made perfect sense. The winner controlled the territory or determined who got to use a playground or what corner store was off limits for the other group.

"A Rock War?" Sean asked. "I…I don't know," he stammered.

"What's a matter, you chicken?" Mike asked, followed by Matt making clucking sounds.

"I am not chicken!" Sean screamed when the taunting became too much. "You name the time and place."

"Well, not on this street," Matt said. "I don't want any parents breaking it up."

"And not on my street," Sean said. "Same reason."

"Fine," Mike said, "let's do it two blocks over on Beechnut."

"Everyone agree?" Matt asked. Then, when no one said a word, he added, "Be there in 15 minutes. And bring your own rocks."

Sean, ensnared by his own devices, jumped on his bike and started to ride away to gather reinforcements. He yelled back over his shoulder, "You're dead!" but we were already scrambling to find rocks.

It was assumed you wouldn't bring any rocks that were big enough to kill anyone, plus you wouldn't be able to throw them too far, but still kids grabbed some big rocks. With our pockets stuffed and bulging, it was an uncomfortable ride to Beechnut. It still amazes me that kids would just go along with the idea of stoning people in the streets without so much as a complaint or a concern, but that was the power Matt and Mike had. They said it, we did it, because we wanted to be cool like them.

When we got to Beechnut, Sean was just coming around the corner. He had managed to get a few more kids, but he was still outnumbered. The one thing he did have was someone's older brother. This kid had to be in high school and he looked like a giant compared to the rest of the group. If the rest of us were scared, it didn't faze Matt. He stepped forward and asked, "You ready?"

Sean must have planned on us running when we saw the big kid, so he turned around and started talking to his gang before answering. Finally he answered, "Yeah, we're ready! Just say when!"

Apparently he didn't know Matt and Mike very well at all. Most kids probably would figure no one would want to take the first shot. Not them. Both of them were excellent shots and in unison hurled the first stones. Thwack! Thwack! Two direct hits. The first screams of pain. The calls of "I'm hit, I'm hit!" And then the floodgates opened. The first barrage was simultaneous. Kids who were really only there to someday say they were there, found themselves chucking stones. Before the first rocks rained down, the bigger kids were releasing a second volley.

The screams were terrible from both sides. Kids were crying and ducking for cover. There was a car near us that took the brunt of the second wave if only because kids were scrambling to get behind it, under it, anywhere out of harm's way. Both sides started to flee, some running, some grabbing their bikes. It was an eerie calm that came over me, the air full of screams: "I'm bleeding!" "Why? Why?" "Run Away!" The shouts were all around me but they became distant, far away sounds like in a dream sequence from a movie. Matt and Mike stood their ground, determined to hold the line as the sheer volume of rocks dissipated until there were none. Sean lay, thirty feet away, on the ground clutching his bloody nose while one of his friends tried to drag him out of the street. Our war had drawn the neighborhood moms out of their houses where they screamed at us to stop and threatened that they had called the police. But who could have called anyone in that time? The entire thing lasted less than a minute.

As kids fled in both directions, we started to jump and cheer. Then, as I turned to watch Sean flee, I spotted the giant high schooler bearing down on us. He closed to within ten feet, clearly on a suicide mission. I threw my rock as hard as I could, not thinking, not aiming, and caught him square in the forehead. He fell.

His screams were worse than any I'd heard before, I'd later describe it a as cross between a dying sheep and a wolverine, and it startled me enough that I didn't realize at first that he had thrown back at us. Matt and Mike stared at me in disbelief.

"Look at your eye!" Matt said.

"Man, he could have killed you!" Mike said.

"What are you talking about?" I asked them.

Then I felt the sting. Right above my eyebrow was starting to swell. It was a goose egg where the giant had hit me with his throw. I had taken him out, but he had got me, too. Matt's head was bleeding and Mike's arm had a welt the size of a tennis ball. The street was deserted except for a couple of moms still yelling and the distant sounds of kids screaming as they escaped.

"Your eye needs ice," Mike said. "And we need to get out of here before the cops show up!"

"Yeah," Matt said, "and my head doesn't feel so good, either."

We had taken the street, we had won the war, but it was not without us paying a steep price. We mounted up on our bikes and rode off, to heal up and celebrate our glorious victory. All the way back to their house, Matt and Mike told me I was a hero, that kids would talk about what we did forever. It was no small thing for a third grader to best a high school kid. This was a day filled with stories for all of us. They promised that after we cleaned up we'd go to Lengel's Market and they'd buy me a Coke.

"Everyone will be there," Mike said, "waiting to hear our stories. Especially since most of them booked before it was over."

As we walked into my cousins' house and headed to the kitchen, my aunt stopped us. She was holding two pee soaked sheets.

"Would you boys like to explain this?" she said. "Your father is not going to be happy when he gets home."

My cousins' faces said it all. They were busted, no surprise from their father, no baseball game or amusement park. Then my aunt turned to me with a look of genuine surprise.

"What happened to your eye?" she asked.

I looked over at my cousins. "Nothing," I said, "I just fell."

SHARPSHOOTER

His eye fixed clearly on his target. His grip was sure and his hand steady. The only way to describe him was deadly accurate. One shot, one hit. No misses. Ever. It did not matter if one expected it or not; he would find a way, swift and silent, to complete his assignment.

I remember clearly the day it happened. It had been a normal morning in the fourth grade – we did some math, we read a story, we did some worksheets. And then, like every day, we went to lunch. I didn't have the good fortune to bring my lunch that day, so I had to buy. It was hamburger day, which wasn't too awful except the hamburgers were kept in steam trays for hours, making them both hard and rubbery, like very flat hockey pucks. They were served up with tater tots, which I did not like at all. Tater tots are an acquired taste I discovered, something I would not truly appreciate until I was in high school years later. At least there was chocolate milk, a faithful stand-by, the one thing a kid could count on no matter how a day was going.

I moved my peach colored plastic tray through the line and walked toward the boys' end of the long cafeteria table reserved for Mrs. Philip's fourth grade class. I was thinking about one of my friends who always brought his lunch and how I could trade him my tater tots for his Twinkies. This guy loved tater tots, probably because he never bought his lunch and considered them an exotic food. I set my tray on the table and started to sit down, when I heard something whiz past my left ear. It struck a third grader with a thwacking noise I was unaccustomed to hearing. I was a veteran of numerous food fights, but I could not place the sound. Food fights normally broke out on mashed potato and gravy day.

It was nasty business, hurling potatoes and gravy across the cafeteria, but it provided the biggest mess without question. Mashed potatoes hit with a sploshing sound. Tater tots, although deadly accurate, generally bounced off a target with no damage and little effect, thus defeating the purpose of attacking an enemy with food. Hamburgers could inflict some damage, enough to make a six or seven year old cry, but they were too Frisbee-like in flight and could easily veer off course.

The sound was unlike anything I had heard and the response immediate. The third grader clutched the back of his neck and let out a little yelp, a cry of surprise and the sting of a sharp pain mixed together. A blotch of red was widening out on the boy's neck as he turned to stare at our table.

"Who did that?" he asked.

"Turn around and go back to your table third grader," Max, who was sitting next to me, said.

"I'm going to tell on you for that," the third grader said as tears started to well up in his eyes.

"You do and you won't see fourth grade," Max said. "Besides, I didn't do anything so who are you going to tell on?"

The third grader knew he was defeated. Max was right. No one had seen anything. The kid went back to his lunch and I turned around to look at my friends at the table.

"What just happened?" I asked.

Max looked at me and smiled. I knew something was up. Three or four boys huddled in closer to hear what he was going to say.

"This morning, on the bus, I was sitting next to Hal. He was saying how he could hit any kid anywhere with a rubber band, hard enough to make him cry. Guess what? He wasn't lying. He can do it."

We all turned and looked across the table at Hal, who sat there staring at us with a smirk. Hal was a non-factor in our world up until now. He was not a primary player or even a secondary one. He was more of a tertiary player, a third string, last tier type of guy. He was the last boy picked before the girls were picked and one time he was even picked for basketball after Jennifer Lupino, who had gone through a growth spurt and was now four inches taller than any boy in our class. Hal batted ninth, played right field, and sat the bench. And now, out of nowhere, he stepped into the spotlight. If a student was caught for instigating a food fight, it meant a whole week of no recess. Instead of playing kickball, you had to help Earl, the million year old janitor, wash down tables with some funky bleach solution and rags that looked like they were old gym shirts. Sure, you had a moment of glory, but the cost was high, making food fights infrequent.

What Hal had done was different though. It was quiet and looked deceptively easy. There was no mess to clean up; it was fast and efficient. Even if the rubber band was found, it could have come from anywhere. There were millions of rubber bands in schools. Pinpointing the source was nearly impossible, unlike a flying lump of mashed potatoes. The only one who even saw Hal do it was Max, and that was because he was watching for it. Hal had waited for the perfect moment, when I screened his shot by stepping in front of him, and then had acted without hesitation to accomplish his task. This brought a new element to elementary school life. Entire grade levels could be brought into line by the fear of this new weapon. Where did it come from? Who would it strike next? The possibilities seemed endless. Stephen Perry's simple invention to hold loose papers together was now in the hands of someone who saw its true potential and was not afraid to unleash the fury of its kinetic energy on an unsuspecting population.

I noticed all of us were staring at Hal in awe, thinking of what this new discovery meant. Hal just stared back, not saying a word, holding that same smirk, knowing that his time had finally come.

It did not surprise me that Hal was not babbling about his talent. He rarely said anything anyway. He almost never spoke in class, unless the teacher called on him, and he almost never said anything important to any of us guys. It was like he was happy just to be around. He was not the kid who was picked on for no reason, that was Chad, but he was not a guy who got any attention either. In fact, as I looked at him at that moment, I realized I knew almost nothing about him and my guess was that neither did anyone else.

His eyes were dark and deep set, but behind those eyes I could tell he had plenty to say if ever given the opportunity. He was short for a fourth grader and a little bit younger than most of us because his birthday was in May or June. I knew he didn't live with his parents because they were both in the army. I think he used to live with them until they were both re-stationed. I think he saw his mom every school break. Either he went to where she was or sometimes she came here when she had leave. I wasn't real sure about his dad, although I remembered a report he read once about his dad being a soldier and a hero in Vietnam. I remembered it because it was the first time I ever heard the word "gook" used. The teacher corrected him, told us it was not a polite term to use, and asked us "to refrain from using that word." Naturally, that meant everyone used that word whenever out of earshot of the teacher until it was replaced by another linguistic fad.

Hal lived with his grandparents, his mother's parents, in a duplex around the corner from Joe's Pizza. They were nice, but they were old, in their sixties, which seemed ancient even compared to my grandparents who were in their late fifties. All I remember thinking is that Hal's grandfather must cut his lawn every day in the summer because anytime I rode past it on my bicycle, he was outside sweeping grass off of the sidewalk.

The house was well-maintained, always painted and clean. In the spring and through the summer, Hal's grandmother would work in the flowerbeds in the yard while Hal washed the family car in the driveway. That's how he earned his allowance, I guessed. When he finished that, Hal would show up wherever everyone was playing and join in, quietly, as if he was always there and he belonged.

Hal's Uncle Jimmy lived in the other side of the duplex. He was not quite right. He had been in the military, but he came home disabled. He looked normal to me but there were rumors that he did not always act normal. My grandfather referred to him as shellshocked one time, and although I did not truly comprehend what that meant, at least it gave me an idea of what was wrong. Most days Uncle Jimmy would work on his car or even throw a football around with Hal in the street. But he never went to work. He never went anywhere, except to drive down to the gas station for cigarettes or to the auto parts store for sparkplugs and oil. Hal never talked about Uncle Jimmy.

When the bell rang for recess a few minutes later, I had not even touched my lunch. I quickly gobbled down my hamburger and chocolate milk and tossed out my tater tots. No Twinkies today - no time to barter. I hurried out onto the playground with all of my friends, who already formed a circle around Hal and were asking him to show off his quick draw move. Hal was thoroughly enjoying the attention. I think that for the first time in his life he had the feeling of being the very best at something, the envy of his peers.

"Show us how you do it, Hal," Max said.

"Yeah. Shoot someone like you did that other kid," Mark added.

The anticipation was building. No one was entirely convinced that what Hal had done in the cafeteria could be duplicated on the playground. Hal didn't speak. Instead, he sighted his next target. He dropped his hands inside his jeans. Two girls with pigtails came running by not ten feet from our circle. The girls looked like twins, but were only friends. In eleventh grade they would both want the same boy to take them to the Junior Prom. When he chose one over the other, they never spoke again. Today, they were still best friends unaware of what was about to happen.

In an instant, Hal had drawn his hands out and fired, one smooth motion that resulted in two direct hits. The girls were stunned. They both screamed. The first girl thought a bee had stung her. She was allergic to bees and went into a panic. Her friend started to cry but stopped when she noticed a rubber band on the ground. She glared at our circle, whispered to her hysterical look-alike, and they ran off to the monkey bars.

We were in awe. It was like something out of a movie. Billy the Kid, Wild Bill Hickock, Buffalo Bill, John Wayne, Clint Eastwood – none of them could match Hal Edinger for speed or accuracy. Within two days, every boy in our class had his pockets full of rubber bands. In three days it was the entire grade. Every house was emptied of ammo. The most daring boys swiped rubber bands from the teacher's desk. I found out that the mailman had an unlimited supply.

School became very tense. Everyone was armed by the end of the week. Firing a shot meant retaliation was imminent. At home, each night, all of the boys honed their skills by shooting empty soda cans, pets, and sisters. We were all at different levels, but we were all dangerous. Outside, on the playground, at the end of the first week, a boy stepped up and challenged Hal. He was good, real good. And fast, too. But at close range in a light spring drizzle, Hal showed why he was the best. The kid got off one shot, glancing off Hal's arm. Hal hit the kid six times, twice between the eyes, once in the ear, and three times in the back of the head as the kid ran away. No one challenged him again.

A cold war developed. No one wanted to suffer humiliation the way the kid did who challenged Hal. The teachers could sense something was wrong, but no one would talk. That would break the code. By the second week of the armed conflict, the teachers knew something was up. There were no rubber bands anywhere. Hal's reputation was still growing. There was talk of the girls starting a revolution. And then it happened- someone squealed.

Word spread on the way to the cafeteria that the principal knew what was going on and he was going to punish everyone involved. Hundreds of rubber bands were thrown into the trash. Countless more got flushed down toilets. By mere fate, Mrs. Philips' fourth grade class got to the cafeteria first, ahead of the message to disarm or face the wrath of Mr. Lockwood. As we sat down to eat, the first whispers came our way that we should dump our rubber bands. Not one of us would listen. We saw through these rumors to the truth, the truth that if we emptied our pockets then we were open for attack on the playground. Death would rain down from above and everyone would laugh at us for falling for a Trojan horse scam.

Ten minutes later, we seriously regretted our poor decision. Mr. Lockwood stormed into the cafeteria, two pig-tailed girls in tow. They pointed at our table. Mr. Lockwood dismissed all of the girls for recess and then went table to table making the boys pull their pockets out. He dismissed the boys, one group at a time, until we were the only ones left, thirteen boys from Mrs. Philips' fourth grade class.

"Stand up boys," Mr. Lockwood said.

We were terrified. The man was huge, especially to a ten year old. No one had been able to move, aware that this was coming, realizing there was no longer any way to dispose of the contents of our pockets.

"Turn your pockets out and put your things on the table in front of you."

One by one, we emptied out our pockets, each of us amassing a pile of rubber bands directly in front of us. Mr. Lockwood turned a bright red and spittle formed in the corners of his mouth. In the empty cafeteria, the only sound I remember was the sound of his breathing. I understood the meaning of rage. The storm of words blended into one ferocious growl. Mark Connors started to cry. The rest of us just looked down at the table.

As he moved down the table and bawled each one of us out, Mr. Lockwood explained the magnitude of our sins and the horrific accidents we had narrowly avoided. He stopped in front of Hal, suddenly looking even angrier. From the middle of his rubber band pile he retrieved a paper clip. It was complete coincidence that Hal had stuffed it in his pocket, but to Mr. Lockwood it was the ultimate weapon. A paperclip, combined with a rubber band, equaled instant blindness. This was gross misconduct. An example had to be made of Hal. Mr. Lockwood sent him to his office while he finished with the rest of us.

We were given a chance to tell on anyone else we knew was involved with the rubber band war. No one said a word. There was nothing worse than ratting out your friends and breaking the code. The twelve of us stood condemned but we would not drag anyone else down. We had our honor.

"You boys have two weeks of lunch detention, no playground, and you'll help Earl clean the cafeteria after lunch." With those words Mr. Lockwood stormed out of the cafeteria.

In all, we got off pretty easy. Lunch detention was not that bad. Sure, it was spring and we wanted to be outside. Hal got five days of out of school suspension. That didn't seem like punishment either; it was more like vacation. We helped sell snacks while the P.T.A. moms supervised us. They stood and drank coffee, gossiped, and occasionally glanced in our direction. Then we all helped Earl wash down the tables and sweep up the floor. After the first week, Mr. Lockwood softened up and gave us each an ice cream sandwich when we finished, so it was like we were being paid.

Hal returned and did lunch detention the second week with us. He was back to his old quiet self, there but not there, practically invisible. Within a month things were back to normal. Hal faded further into the background. At some point he was no longer in the class photo. I heard he transferred to a Catholic school with an ROTC program before ninth grade.

The summer before I left for college I briefly dated a girl who graduated from a Catholic school. One afternoon when we were lounging by her pool, she brought out her yearbook to show me some pictures. As I flipped through her yearbook, I saw him. He was dressed in his full ROTC uniform, looking very serious, no smile on his face.

"I know him," I said pointing at his photo.

"Really?" she answered. "He was the funniest guy in the whole school."

KILLER HILL

The first flakes of snow to fall always brought tremendous excitement to everyone in school. It signaled a change from the miserable damp brown of late fall to the cold but glorious white of winter. It also meant new outdoor activities, like skating, hockey, and especially sledding. What could be better than rushing down some steep slope, dodging trees, only a piece of plastic between your face and the icy death beneath you? The only problem: this was not the Rocky Mountains. None of our sledding runs came close to matching our visions of what it could be like if we had an actual mountain. Except one. The hill was, on three sides, a family friendly good time. It was fast at the top but gentle enough that parents with younger children could also sled there. Sure, we built jumps and tried to make it more dangerous, but it still was tame. But not on the fourth side, the back side, where no one but the bravest of the brave dared go: Killer Hill.

What made Killer Hill so dangerous? I mean, why call a hill "killer" in the first place unless someone got killed? That was the question I had, until I heard the story from the most reliable source of all, my dad. Every time I went sledding my father would say, "Have fun. But don't let me catch you going down Killer Hill. A kid died on that, you know."

I would answer, "Sure dad," and go off on my way but I wasn't sure at all. In fact, I was pretty sure no one had ever died on Killer Hill but everyone's parents said the same thing to keep you off of it. I was tempted on more than one occasion to just go down it to prove everyone wrong, except when you got to the top, it was scary. I believed you had to be crazy to even try it, so me and my friends never did.

Then, it finally happened. My friend Jason had his cousin visiting him from Kansas. I'm almost sure there are no hills in Kansas because whenever we did maps of the U.S. in school we just colored Kansas in brown to represent wheat and corn or barley. It was just a flat brown spot on the map where no one ever went except Dorothy and the first thing she did was try to get out of there. I'm still not sure why she ever went back. I used to think she probably got killed by another tornado the next day. That would serve her right, too. She was wanted for murdering that witch and she wasn't even sorry for it, let alone ditching all of her friends and letting them clean up the mess. Anyway, Jason's cousin showed up on mid-winter break, in February, and his name was Don. It was short for Donald but Jason said not to call him that because he hated it and he would cry and Jason would get in trouble.

In reality, everything made Donald upset. He was a big baby. Worse, he never shut up. He went on and on about how great Kansas was and why where we lived stunk. So that's why we talked him into going down Killer Hill.

"You'll be a legend," I told him, which was true, but I left out the part that he would probably die. Everyone backed me up, plus we kept telling Donald how a real Kansas cowboy should be the first to conquer the hill. Now, we did not actually think he would go through with it. Like the rest of us who had stood on the brink of the precipice, we were certain he would chicken out and run away. He almost did, too. He was terrified. So when we started telling him he was chicken, we knew he wanted to run. To this day I'm almost positive if Ronny Hobart hadn't said what he said, then Donald would have walked back down the hill.

"That proves it. All you Kansas queers are a bunch of sissies!" Ronny yelled at him.

The look on Donald's face was pure determination. He jumped on his sled, screamed "Yahoo!" and promptly crashed into a tree. He had made it half-way down, which was still more than anyone I had ever seen. Killer Hill was steep, so it took a while to walk down and drag Donald back up. Then we had to take turns pulling him back to Jason's house on the sled, Donald crying and screaming that his arm was broken the whole way. When we got there, Jason's mom and aunt came out so we all took off. Jason didn't get to come out and play for the rest of the vacation because he had to stay inside and wait on Donald, who had broken his arm in two places. We didn't miss Donald, but still it was pretty brave of him to try and conquer the hill.

The next day after my father, and every other parent in the neighborhood, heard about Donald's accident, he sat me down for a talk.

"What happened?" he asked.

"Well, the guys and I..."

"You didn't have anything to do with this, did you?"

"Well, sort of but we didn't think he'd do it," I answered.

"You encouraged him to do it? How many times have I told you to stay off that hill?"

"But Dad, no one has ever gone down before..."

"No one has gone down? I told you a boy was killed on that hill."

"But everybody says that. Who was the boy? When did it happen?"

"The boy was my neighbor. He lived four houses down

the road. He was a few years older than me. I went to his funeral."

"You mean, it's real? A kid actually died? And you knew him? How did it happen? Did he hit a tree?"

"It was a long time ago, when I was little. There were no trees back then and sometimes kids went down the hill. But then one night, this boy, my neighbor went down. His friends had built a jump at the bottom. He went over the jump and died."

I was stunned. It was all real. Wait until I told the guys. And I would wait. For my part in Donald's crash, I was grounded for the rest of vacation, with extra chores. I also got to go apologize to Donald and bring him some comic books and a card that I paid for out of my allowance.

By the time I was un-grounded, we had a spring thaw and the sledding was done. But I kept thinking about Killer Hill and how that kid died. We could have sent ol' Donald to his death. In a way, it was lucky he hit that tree since it probably saved his life.

In the spring, Ronny's mom got married again. When Ronny was seven his dad died from cancer and for the last couple of years his family had it tough. But his new step-dad was pretty nice, even taking Ronny's friends for burgers and ice cream a couple times. We knew he was just trying to get in good with Ronny, but it was fun anyway so we enjoyed it while it lasted.

Ronny was one of my best friends before his mom got remarried. Then, that summer, Ronny's new step-sister came to stay with her dad, and Ronny became everyone's best friend. His step-sister, Jennifer, was gorgeous. She was already a teenager, and she knew we all would do whatever she wanted. She had dark hair and dark eyes and she got so tan that summer; she seemed absolutely exotic. She had a funny little accent because she was from Connecticut and it drove us wild. She didn't pay for a Coke or an ice cream cone the whole summer. When the end of August rolled around every boy in the neighborhood was heartbroken except Ronny, who was glad to see her go. She said she would be back right after Christmas to stay for the school break. We started counting down the days.

When school let out in December, we were as excited as ever. It snowed almost every day for a week, not a lot, but it was starting to add up. The day after Christmas it snowed enough to really start sledding, so we were back on Killer Hill.

When I left the house that morning, my father said, "Have fun. But don't let me catch you going down Killer Hill. A kid died on that, you know."

I answered, "Sure dad," but this time I knew he wasn't kidding. I also knew what the punishment would be for disobeying him.

When I got to the hill there were already a ton of kids there, breaking in their new sleds, having fun. Everyone was basically split into groups according to age, so all my friends were sledding together down the side farthest from all the little kids with their parents.

"Check out my new sled," Jason said.

"Check out Ronny's sister," Mark answered.

And there she was, looking absolutely perfect, just the way I remembered her, only older, better, more mature. I had thought for months about what I would say to her when I saw her again. I pictured how smooth I would be, how she would laugh and toss her perfect hair, how I would ask her to go for a milkshake at the Dairy-Del.

"Hey," Jennifer said snapping me from my trance, "I said hello. Are you ignoring me or did you just forget who I am?"

So I was a daydreaming idiot. Real smooth. "What? No, hey, sorry. I was just thinking of, uh, um, something else. So, hello." Did I sound like a complete moron or what? At that moment I was ready to die. If I could crawl under something and hide, I would have.

"If you're done hitting on my sister, we built a wicked jump down here you might want to try out," Ronny said.

"I wasn't hitting on her, I was just saying hi."

"Whatever. Let's go dufus. By the way, she has a boyfriend in Connecticut."

Since I was completely embarrassed now, and since Jennifer heard everything Ronny said, I just took off down the hill. The jump was cool, they did a good job building it, and we had a blast all day trying to find new ways to outdo each other.

By the late afternoon all the younger kids and their parents had gone home and the hill was basically ours. That's when we started trying new stunts. I got Jason to lie at the end of a jump and then jumped over him. Then I kept adding people until it was pure Evel Kneival. I was up to six kids and going for seven, sure that this would impress Jennifer, when I realized she wasn't watching. She wasn't even around.

"Hey, Ronny, where's your sister?" I asked. "She won't want to miss this."

"First, I don't think she cares. Second, she's up on top of the hill somewhere, probably talking to some other boy."

This made me angry, not just because Ronny was trying to make me upset, but because I realized that it might be true. I tromped up the hill to find out and found Jennifer looking down Killer Hill.

"How come no one sleds here?" she asked.

"That's Killer Hill," I answered, "no one goes down there. A kid died on that, you know."

"Really? He died? Did you see it?" she asked.

"No. But I saw the last kid that tried it. He didn't make it. He broke his arm. We carried him screaming all the way home."

"No way."

Just then everybody else showed up and started telling stories of Killer Hill. Jennifer listened, wide-eyed, taking it all in.

"…and that's why no one will ever make it down this hill alive," Ronny finished saying. We all had to agree with him. All of us except Jennifer.

"You mean none of you have ever tried it?" she asked. "Not one?"

"Jennifer, I just explained how you will die if you try it. No one has even made it more than halfway down, and that kid broke his arm bad," Ronny told her.

"Just because no one has done it doesn't mean it can't be done. I can't believe none of you has the guts to try it. I know lots of guys back home who would do this in a minute, just to be the first to say they did it."

"Well, then the guys you know must be stupid because they would all be dead," Jason said.

"They're not stupid," she said. "They just aren't babies like you boys."

The emphasis on "boys" was both obvious and painful. She took her shot at all of us and we all flinched. She was crazy. She had no idea what she was really saying. If you go down Killer Hill, you die. End of discussion.

The sky was turning purple on the horizon as the sun set. It was getting colder and soon it would be dark. We'd all go home and eat dinner with our families. Tomorrow this would all be forgotten. The wind started to blow and swirl the snow in little vortexes on top of the hill. They looked like little tornados. Like they have in Kansas.

"I'll do it," I said. There was a collective gasp.

"Are you crazy?" Jason asked.

"You don't need to impress my sister," Ronny said. "Come on, man. Let's forget this and go home."

"Did you forget my cousin last year? Do you want to end up in a tree? Only maybe you'll break your head open instead," Jason pleaded.

It was all very good reasoning. But now I was committed. I understood what none of us did when Donald took the leap – this was not for them, it was for me. Yes it's true; I wanted to impress Jennifer, too. I wanted to show her that I was better than the Connecticut boys, whoever they were. Mostly, I wanted to prove this could be done.

I lined up my sled to go between two large trees, one of

which Donald had run into. If I could get past them, it was an almost clear shot to the bottom. At the bottom, if you made it, you had to slow down somehow or bail out before you hit the large drainage ditch that ran parallel to an access road that led to a storage building for snow equipment. Since snowplows were going over that road all the time, the road was always bare. If you somehow jumped the ditch, hitting that pavement would result in eating asphalt. So not only was the hill steep so you gained speed quickly, you had to avoid trees, rocks, a ditch, and the road. I took a deep breath and thought of my father's warning. "Don't let me catch you going down Killer Hill. A kid died on that, you know."

"Wait!" Jennifer said. "I'm going with you."

I was in shock. "What?" I said.

"I want to go, too," she said again and jumped in the sled with me.

"Are you kidding me?" Ronny asked. "No way. No way. I am not letting you kill yourself. Get out of that sled."

"Sorry little brother. I'm doing this."

"If you get hurt, I'll get blamed. Jennifer, please get out of the sled." Ronny was serious. He was genuinely concerned but she didn't care.

"Let's do this," she giggled. "It's so scary!"

In my life I have done some really stupid things to impress a girl. Over time, I have been able to justify, rationalize, validate, and defend myself for what I did. But this, this was just dangerous and stupid. I looked down the hill and begged God to help me survive. I promised all sorts of things that I swore I would fulfill. I saw all the way down the hill, between the trees to the ditch and the road. It was insane. Then I felt Jennifer pressed against me. I could smell her hair. There were only two pairs of snow pants between us and she was holding on tightly to my legs. I couldn't breathe. Was it her or my impending death?

I thought again of the boy who died when my father was young. There were a lot of unanswered questions right at that moment. How did he really die? What was he thinking right before he went down? Years later, when I was in college, I thought about these questions one night while working on a term paper. I was feeling kind of fried, so I took a break and looked up the event in the files. I found the newspaper article. My dad had been twelve, ironically enough. The boy was actually seventeen. He and his friends had been out drinking and decided to go sledding at 2 a.m. It was a snowstorm. The picture in the paper of the hill showed no trees. It was a straight shot to the bottom. The drainage ditch was also added later. The teenager, Harry Ague, had gone straight down the hill and into the road. A snowplow was on its way back to the storage garage. The driver never saw him. These are things I did not know at the time. I also didn't know if I would ever be this close to a girl again. Or that Jennifer was never going to break up with her Connecticut boyfriend to be with me.

"Hold on tight," I told her.

"Don't do it. Just don't do it," Jason pleaded. Everyone else was eerily silent.

I pushed off, but as we sped up, everything became slow motion. The extra weight in the sled made it pull left and just for a minute I thought we'd hit the trees. I leaned right, pulling Jennifer with me and we passed through the trees. We were gaining speed at an incredible rate, the ditch and the road rushing up at us. There were a number of big rocks that were covered in snow and we hit one, going airborne and slamming down, almost rolling over but straightening out as I dragged my hands to act as a rudder. In another second we would hit the ditch. I was surprised how incredibly calm I was considering the end was near, and again I pulled Jennifer right turning the sled hard to do a sideways hockey stop, kicking powder up over us, slowing down, slowing down, slowing down, and we flipped into the ditch.

The ditch was filled with fresh powder and we sank into it. I landed on top of Jennifer, who still had her eyes shut tight, and then she slowly opened them. I could hear everyone cheering and yelling from the top of the hill. In a minute they would be here to check on us, wondering if we survived the final fall. Buried by powder, pressed close to Jennifer who looked angelic with her hair full of snow, she smiled at me and said, "Are we dead?"

"If we are, then this is heaven."

She laughed, pulled me close, and kissed me.

ELEVATOR BABIES

I was about twelve years old the first time I met him. He was new to the neighborhood and I sized him up as being around ten or eleven. He seemed out of place and nervous about having to wait there on the curb without anyone to talk to, so he just kind of stared up at the sky, like the clouds were the most interesting thing he had ever seen. I decided I would go over and talk to him, I mean, after all, this was my bus stop. I was the oldest one there, a sixth grader and everything, and I definitely ran the show. This was my turf and all of the kids were my people.

"Hey kid! What's your name?" I asked as I strolled over to check him out.

"Who? Me?" he asked.

I rolled my eyes, really exaggerating my irritation for effect, and said, "Yeah you. Who else would I be talking to, sport?"

I hated it whenever anyone called me sport. I don't know why, it just rubbed me wrong. Mr. Johnson, who ran the small engine and appliance repair shop down the block, called me sport. Adults always did things like that. Maybe they thought kids liked it. Maybe no one ever told them to stop doing it. But that didn't matter because I decided to call him sport. I wanted answers from this kid before things got hostile. He'd invaded my turf.

"My name's...uh," he stuttered.

"Uh what? D'you forget your name or something, kid?"

"No way, José! My name's Jonathon Alan VanHatten III. I'm new here. Just moved to the neighborhood!"

What did he think I was, an idiot? Of course he was new here. I'd never seen him before, he had to be new. He did have spunk though. That I liked. He didn't just take my crap; he stood up for himself. That made him okay in my book.

"Well Jonathon Alan VanHatten III, it's nice to meet you. The only problem is there are already too many people named Jonathon, or John, or Johnny in this neighborhood and VanHatten is too long. How about I just call you "V." That sounds like a pretty cool nickname to me and no one will get you confused with anyone else."

"Yeah, okay, I guess so," V said.

I could tell the sudden name change was something he'd have to get used to, but that was life. Within two minutes he'd lost his identity and wherever he was from didn't matter anymore. Now, he was part of this neighborhood, part of my crew.

It didn't take long for V to fit in. He played Wiffle ball with all of the guys after school, and he wasn't even that bad. Apparently he'd played before in his old neighborhood. He fit in so well that it wasn't long before the guys and I really started razzing him like we did each other.

V made a pretty easy target, too. He was shorter than most kids his age, wore his hair full of gel or hairspray or something that made it stick a good five or six inches off his head in some ridiculous way that he swore was in style, and to top it all off he had a really big nose. No, it was more than a nose. It was a "schnoz." When you saw it you just wanted to say, "Look at the size of that schnoz!"

When I finally did ask him about it, after the guys put me up to it, I came right out and said, "Why is your nose so freakin' huge?" and all of the fellas broke out laughing hysterically.

"My nose isn't so big," he said. "My face just has to grow into it still!"

That was it. He left an opening for everyone to take a shot. He could have just said, "Shut up!" or "Oh yeah, real funny!" but instead he set himself up. Then the jokes started to fly. Jokes about his mother giving birth to him – "Congratulations! It's a nose!"- and how many tissue boxes it would take to stop his sneeze. Nothing too terrible, but for an eleven year old, it was enough to shake V up.

"I think I have to go home and babysit my brother," V said. "I'll see you all later."

It was official, V was initiated. He took his humiliation and ran home with it. Tomorrow, everything would be forgotten and we'd all be friends again. At that age it had to be that way or else you sat home by yourself and sulked. If you did that, you didn't get to play ball and that was worse than getting the chicken pox during summer vacation. Everyone knew it, everyone accepted it, and V was no exception because he was part of the crew.

After about two weeks of V suddenly having to run home and babysit his brother every time things got hot, he decided to start teasing the other guys back. He was pretty smart about it, too. He always sided with the biggest guy, which was me whenever I was around. About this same time I started to find out more about V. For a younger kid he sure knew a lot and I was impressed.

One day we started talking about our families and what our dads did and who made more money and who had the greatest dad ever. Everyone laid it on pretty thick, but V kept quiet.

"So what does your dad do, V?" I asked. "Or is he a bum?"

"My dad's got a great job," V said.

"Oh yeah? What's so great about it?"

"Well, my dad gets to drive all of the heavy equipment for the town. You know, street sweepers, garbage trucks, the whole deal."

"Whoa, that's cool! You mean your dad gets to drive all that stuff? He picks up my garbage? That's the best job ever! Think of all the cool stuff people throw out!"

Everyone was in agreement; V's dad had the best job. No one could top being the town street sweeper and garbage man. That was success. That was making it big time. It would be a long time before the idea of being a cop and having a gun would start to make us think differently. For now, V had impressed everyone and he knew it.

"Yeah, my dad practically runs this entire town," V went on, "He does it all. He's even thinking of running for mayor. He's always saying he'd do a better job."

"So, wait a minute, V," I interrupted. "Your dad really rides on the garbage truck?"

"That's what I keep saying. Drives it, rides on it, works the trash compactor, even hauls it to the dump."

The guys couldn't contain themselves.

"Holy moly!"

"He goes to the dump, too?"

"No way. No way!"

"Of course he goes to the dump! Gets to find all sorts

of neat stuff. Brings home all sorts of cool things!" V was loving this. He had everyone's attention. The ice cream truck could have come by with the driver throwing Nutty Buddys out the window and no one would have cared.

Another one of the guys jumped in. "V, you're telling me that your dad not only rides on the truck, works the trash compactor, and goes to the dump, but he also gets to find stuff and bring it home? You're full of it! Nobody gets to do all that and get paid!"

It was getting to be too much. This was a dream job. To boys like us, the dump was magical. Did people even realize what went on there? People threw away bicycles. And things that could be turned into go-carts. And random metal objects that just looked cool. The possibilities were endless.

"You think that's cool," V said, "my dad also gets to go into the sewers and fix things sometimes."

This blew everyone away. The chance to go down into the sewers was totally unbelievable. All of those tunnels, all of the stories about what went on down there. In the movies, the best action took place when cops chased mobsters through the sewers. It was glamorous.

"So what's it like down there? What does your dad tell you about it, V?"

"Oh man, the stories he tells! Hundred pound man-eating sewer rats, rabid raccoons, dead bodies, everything! Then there's the alligators that…"

A gasp went up from the stunned audience. We were already hooked, but this was a new twist. Rats, yes. Raccoons, of course. Dead bodies, sure, that's reasonable.

But alligators down there? Not in anyone's wildest dreams did they imagine real live alligators.

"You mean your dad sees alligators down there?" one of the guys asked.

"Of course," V said. "There's alligators in the sewers."

"But how did they get there, V?" I asked. Not that I for real, 100% believed him, but I did want to know.

"Well, people bring them home from Florida as pets. Then they flush them down the toilets because they don't want them and then they live down there eating the dead bodies and rats. Everybody knows that," V said.

"Well, sure, but nobody ever gets to see them or anything," I said, a little embarrassed.

"My dad does," V went on. "In fact, last week he was attacked by one. It had to be ten...no eleven...feet long. Enormous teeth. Came right out of the muck, down where you can't see him hiding. It grabbed my dad and pulled him down. Luckily, he had his pipe wrench handy so he clubbed it to death. He said he's thinking of having it stuffed."

"That is the coolest thing I've ever heard," somebody said.

"I can't believe it. You are so lucky," someone else added.

"When can we see it, V? I mean, when is it getting stuffed?" I asked.

"Well, uh, you know, it'll be done soon, if he decides to do it, I mean," V mumbled. "It costs a lot of money to stuff a fourteen foot alligator, and my dad doesn't like to show off or anything."

"I thought you said it was eleven feet long, V?"

"Did I say eleven? I meant fourteen."

"So can we come by and see the carcass or what?"

"Sure, but not today," V said. "I think I have to go home and babysit my brother."

For a few days alligators were the hot topic on the block. There was talk of an expedition into the recesses of the sewer, with V's father guiding us through. That never panned out, and after a few days of waiting to see the dead alligator, V finally told us his mom made his dad take it to the dump because it stunk too badly. Nobody forgot that disappointment, and so we waited until January and gave V a painful reminder that he shouldn't fool around with his friends by convincing him to lick a flagpole. Nobody pointed directly to the alligator incident as the reason for selecting V as flagpole licker, but it was in the back of all of our minds- sufficient motive for his choice as "volunteer."

Still, V wasn't bothered by anything. I think he liked the attention. He kept up with his stories, each one causing us to doubt the truthfulness of them a little more. He'd tell us stories about a kid who didn't listen to his mom's warning to chew with his mouth closed and who choked to death on a bee that flew right down his throat and stung him. Then there was the time we were all going swimming, right after we'd eaten, and V refused to join us.

"You coming in?" I asked V.

"No, not for at least an hour or two," V said. "I had a cousin once who went swimming right after he ate. He got cramps, fell over, and drowned in only about four inches of water."

"V, you sound like my mother," one of the guys heckled.

"I swear it's true!" V shouted. "But hey, it's your life

you're risking. I have to go now anyway. I have to babysit my brother."

This kind of thing went on for nearly two summers without much change. Then one July afternoon when it was almost too hot to do anything, except play ball, but you had to stop for breaks every hour so no one died of heat stroke, we were all sitting under the big maple tree in the park. First we were talking about baseball cards, then about why girls can't play baseball, then just about girls, then about one of the guy's older brothers who had the best looking girlfriend we had ever seen, then about her having his baby. It literally only took three minutes to reach that point.

One of the younger kids, maybe a fifth grader, who just started to hang around with us because even though he couldn't hit, he could play right field, he asked the fateful question.

"Could someone just explain to me where the baby comes from?" he asked. "I mean, my grandmother says the stork, but I'm not stupid."

While we had a good idea, and felt we were on the verge of really understanding this greatest of life's mysteries, not one of us had the answer, exactly. It was obvious this kid didn't watch enough T.V. Everyone knew babies were born in hospitals, even if we weren't totally sure how. But I knew enough to keep the little kid quiet and save face in front of the guys.

"So how are they born?" they asked me.

"Well, you know," I started, buying a little more time to think. "A guy and a girl start doing stuff together, she gets pregnant, and after nine months she goes to the hospital and has a baby."

"Yeah, we know that. But how does she get pregnant?" someone asked.

"Are you crazy? You think I'm going to tell you how? Then you go home and tell your parents, and then they call my parents and ask what's going on with me telling their kid everything about getting pregnant and I end up grounded. Forget it. Ask your own parents if you want to know more! Or else watch more T.V. and get your facts straight."

"All I know," V stated matter-of-factly, "is that ninety percent of all babies are born in elevators."

"How could you possibly know that?" I asked.

"It's a proven fact! How many births have you seen in your life? How many of those births were in elevators? Most of them I'd say. You see at least one a night on T.V. Why? Because that's where women have 'em, that's why."

It was a revelation. Everyone was shocked. V was right. All of the births I'd ever seen were on T.V. and they were almost always in elevators. Sure, occasionally someone had a baby in the back of a cab on the way to the hospital, but usually it was in the hospital elevator. Some doctor or nurse or orderly or janitor would wheel a woman in labor onto the elevator. Somewhere between the lobby and the maternity ward the elevator would stop. It's dark, there's a lot of screaming and confusion, and next thing you know, it's a boy! Or a girl. Or twins. That seemed to happen a lot, too. I looked around at the guys who were looking back at me to confirm this. I couldn't, I just didn't know for sure. There was only one thing to do – call V on it.

"All right, V. If so many babies are born in elevators, why don't we go over and watch one getting born?" I asked.

V was stuck. It was put up or shut up. He looked frantically from one face to the next, looking for anyone to take his side. No one did. He decided to fall back on his best defense.

"I would, but I think I have to go home and babysit my brother," he said as he started to turn and walk away.

"You told us your brother went to your grandparents' house for the week," I answered.

"Oh yeah. I forgot. But I do have to go home. I have some homework to finish up," he tried again.

"It's the middle of July," one of the guys said.

"There's no excuse, V, not to go up to the hospital. Unless, of course, you've been telling stories all along and that would make you a lying, yellow-bellied faker, and a cheater, AND a quitter," I said. The last part was just to put it over the top, but it worked.

"I'll prove it to you. We'll all go up to the hospital and see what's what."

V was cornered. He had no way out. It reminded me of a story my grandfather told me about a beaver gnawing his leg off to get out of a trap. V was either right, or he had better start chewing. No matter what, he had to save face or be teased for months.

There were nine of us headed up towards the hospital once we ditched the younger kids. Nine of us spread across the road on our BMX bikes, popping wheelies, jumping the curb, cutting across small patches of lawn that old women guarded with brooms, getting rowdier and rowdier and putting on a show as we approached our goal – the hospital. In reality, it was all a bluff, we weren't sure we'd get in. None of us had come here without parents before, but we were on a mission. I told everyone that if anyone asked them, they were here to see their grandmother.

We left our bikes in the bushes and immediately everyone volunteered to guard the bikes. In the end, I decided it would be better if we didn't all go in and make a scene, so just V and I went in. I figured, according to everything V said the entire ride over, that this would only take about ten minutes before we'd see a birth.

V wanted to split up, to cover more ground he said, but he wasn't leaving my sight. Three nurses asked us where we were going before we finally found an elevator, but the grandmother idea worked like a charm. After fifteen elevator rides to the top floor and back down I was starting to get anxious. People got on, people got off, but we didn't see one pregnant woman.

"I don't understand," V said. "There should be dozens of them around here! Maybe we got on the wrong elevator."

That seemed to make sense. There were a lot of elevators. I thought maybe we should try another one, but just then the door opened and a doctor stepped in. I looked at V, and he knew what I was thinking. He shook his head and motioned to keep quiet, but I couldn't let this opportunity pass.

"Hey doc. I've got a question for you," I said.

"Certainly, young man. What is it?" he asked.

"Well, you see, I was wondering where all the pregnant women are."

"That would be maternity, son. Fourth floor. Why, is your mommy there?"

"No. We just wanted to see babies being born. Where can we do that?"

The doctor chuckled, but I hadn't said anything funny. This was a mission for us. We wanted to see some serious baby birthing.

"I'm afraid you're going to have to wait until med school before that happens," he said. "Unless, of course, someone gets on and has one in this elevator!"

The doctor laughed out loud, amused by his own joke. I threw a look at V, but he wouldn't look at me. His face was bright red.

"You mean, doctor, that babies don't get born on elevators, like on T.V.?" I asked reluctantly.

"Like on T.V.!" the doctor could not control his laughter. He was hysterical as the bell sounded and the doors opened for his floor. As he stepped out and the elevator doors started to close, all we heard was his laughing and the words, "Hey Nurse Bennett! Wait until I tell you what just…"

V wouldn't look at me. He stared down at his sneakers, expecting me to lay into him good.

"Well, I guess babies aren't born in elevators," I said.

"Guess not," he muttered.

"Awe, don't worry about it V. Everybody screws up sometimes."

"What will the guys say? They're gonna kill me! I'll be a yellow-bellied lying faker and a cheater!"

"And a quitter," I added. "But don't worry. I'll stick up

for you. If anybody starts with you, I'll tell them to shut their trap."

"You will? Oh man, that's great. You're a real pal."

"I always watch out for my friends," I said. "Let's get out of here and go play ball."

"Can I be on your team?"

"Sure. You can even hit first."

V was happy and the guys didn't hate him, although they teased him a little, which was okay because he earned it. Most importantly, V stopped using babysitting his brother as a way out of his stories. Unless, of course, he was absolutely sure his brother was home.

PACKY

The day Jonathan, whom nobody called Jonathan, moved out of the neighborhood was a Thursday. No one, not Ronny or V or anybody, had expected it. They had all found out the night before, when I had gone to my grandparents' house for dinner. It was late when I got home and they had given up trying to call me hours before. No one left a message, so when I showed up on my bike the next morning like always, I had no idea what the U-Haul was doing in Jonathan's driveway,

I skidded to a stop right in front of his house where most of the other guys were already gathered. "What's going on?" I asked.

"He's moving," they all answered at once.

"What? When did they decide to do that? I don't understand. Why are they leaving?"

This was the first time any of our friends had ever moved out of the neighborhood. People moved here, not away. Anytime one of the old timers croaked, a family with kids bought the house and moved in. None of the other guys had any answers. It was an unbelievable, inconceivable thing and everyone was still reeling from the shock.

"Last night," Ronny said, "we were all together having a game of hide and seek in the dark. He showed up and said he was moving and that he had to load the moving van and he left. He looked like he might cry. He didn't say why they were leaving or anything, just that he had to go. We tried calling him but no one answered the phone. Finally, we went down to his house to try and talk to him last night but all his mom said was he was busy and he would see us today to say good-bye before they left."

Just then he came out of the house towards all of us who were waiting in the street. You couldn't mistake him for anyone else, even from ten blocks away. He had bright red hair, cut almost in the shape of a perfect bowl, but with a little extra length so that his ears were hidden. His skin was pale and freckles covered his face. His front tooth was chipped, and he was kind of fat. Most of the time he had on football jerseys, a purple and gold one with 88 printed on it was his favorite, and he wore it at least three times a week. He always wore blue jeans, even on hot summer days like this one, and a pair of grungy old sneakers that never seemed to wear out. He was Jonathan Patrick O'Leary, born on St. Patrick's Day, and nicknamed Packy by his mother from the moment he was born. It was the perfect name to fit him and what everyone called him, from all of his friends, to the teachers in school, to his priest at St. John's church.

He was a permanent fixture in the neighborhood, so you always expected him to be there. We had ridden the bus to school together since kindergarten and counted down the days until we could get our driver's licenses. He wasn't the first person picked whenever we played sports, but he was also never the last. Packy always got more attention than he deserved when his older sister was around. She was three years older than him and much better looking. You know the expression you must have gotten hit by the ugly stick? We used to tease Packy and tell him he got beat by the shillelagh. Twice. His sister was dark haired and beautiful, so we teased him and said he was the real Irish curse.

His family lived right in the middle between my house at the far end of the block and Ronny's house at the other end in a puke green two-story that looked a lot like all of the other houses on the street except the color was worse.

"Hey Packy," we would say, "when you gonna paint your house? It would improve the whole block!"

"Aw, my dad will probably get to it next week," he'd answer.

We knew that he meant never because Packy's dad never got around to doing hardly anything he said he would. Like his dad was always going to take him to a Yankee game or to see the Jets play, but every weekend Packy ended up hanging out with us while his dad sat on the porch and drank beer, Old Milwaukee's Best, cracking one can after another. Packy always had an excuse why he couldn't go, but mostly he'd say that his dad was working too much and just needed to relax that weekend. Packy's mom worked too, nights somewhere, but none of us ever asked about her. I guess we never thought it was that important.

One August Packy joined Pop Warner football, without telling any of us first, so that really surprised us. It shocked us because, even though Packy liked football, he wasn't the best at it. His two favorite sports were WWF wrestling and playing Spud on Saturday mornings. He was too young to be a professional wrestler, but he was sure that when he got older it was probably what he would do.

"My body is in perfect shape for wrestling," he'd always brag. "Just look at me. One hundred fifty pounds of pure American muscle!" and he'd flex his pythons.

Everyone laughed, but we knew that he was a good wrestler whenever we were fooling around. Packy knew all the moves like the atomic knee drop, the figure four leg-lock, and the cobra clutch. He was the only one big enough to do a lot of the moves that required you to pick the other guy up and slam him down on something.

Then there was Spud. All of the kids in the neighborhood loved Spud and anyone could play it. It didn't matter if ten of us played because only one person could lose. I think that's why Packy loved Spud so much – he hardly ever lost a game. But since there was no school Spud team to join, it was more a neighborhood game, Packy chose football.

When it came to football, Packy couldn't throw too well, and he couldn't run real fast, and he didn't catch that well either. Mostly, he always wanted to block or rush and since on the playground no one else really wanted to do those things, he always had a job. Plus, he could count Mississippi's really fast, so no one ever argued with him when he called defensive lineman. Everyone else wanted to play quarterback or wide receiver, so Packy was a pretty important pick for your team.

"What'd you go and join Pop Warner for?" Ronny asked him when we found out. "We play football all the time!"

"I decided I want to be a football player," Packy answered, "but for real. Plus, when you play on the team you get a jersey. I'm number 88. Wait'll the girls at school see me. They love the jocks and always want to wear your jersey and everything."

That made us all think for a minute. Maybe Packy was on to something. The girls, especially the older girls, did seem to like football players, and they always had on their jerseys before games. At twelve, this seemed like the perfect way to get girls to notice you without actually having to talk to them.

"Yeah, but what position are you going to play?" I asked him.

"Probably left bench," V said, and we all laughed.

"Maybe he'll be the water boy," Ronny said, trying to outdo V.

"Yeah, then he can bring everybody water," Chad said.

"Shut up, Chad, or I'll punch your face in you dork!" Packy yelled and then shoved Chad to the ground to show he wasn't kidding. Nobody liked Chad anyway, but he always hung around. Packy just wanted to take the heat off of himself, so he did what any of us would have done.

"Aw, don't start with him Packy," I said. "He's just going to start crying and then have his mother come yell at us again."

"My mother doesn't come…"

"Shut up, Chad!" we yelled in unison, and Chad, fighting to hold back the tears, moved in behind all of the rest of the guys, keeping quiet to avoid getting any more attention.

"You still haven't told us what position you're going to play yet, Packy."

"Well, the coach isn't sure yet, but he'll probably start me on the offensive line."

"I thought only fat kids play on the line," V said.

"He is a fat kid," Ronny said, "just look at him. There's fat rolls coming out from under his jersey!"

"I am not fat!" Packy hollered. "I'm pure American muscle. Made in the U.S.A.," and he flexed his biceps.

"You're right. You're not fat, Packy. And V's nose isn't bigger than Pinocchio's."

V took a swing at Ronny. "You're lucky I missed, Ronny! Next time you're dead!"

Ronny only laughed and turned without warning to grab hold of Packy's gut. "What do you call this?" Ronny asked, shaking the roll.

Packy outweighed Ronny by fifty pounds and just tossed him aside like a chicken wing bone that's been sucked clean. "I'm just husky," Packy said. "I'm husky, and that's what you need to play on the line."

After that, Packy had practice after school every day and games on Saturday mornings. He'd show up at the bus stop with his bruises and cuts, his battle scars he called them, and always with his jersey on. The girls never asked to wear it, and that convinced the rest of us to stay off the team. The pain didn't seem worth the gain.

Eventually, Packy made the modified team, and one morning, about two weeks into the season, he came to the bus stop with his fingers wrapped in tape. It wasn't athletic tape or any other special kind, just ordinary scotch tape, holding two of his fingers together.

"Why do you have scotch tape on your fingers?" V asked him.

"I think I broke one of my fingers," he said. "We only had scotch tape at home. I don't want the coach to find out though. We got a big game this week that I don't want to miss. I heard the J.V. coach was going to be there, to scout for next year's team. It's my big chance to show my skills. I'll just take it off before practice today."

When we heard him say that, there was no doubt that Packy was one of the toughest kids we had ever seen in our lives. He had everyone's sympathy. Maybe we had been wrong, maybe all the practices and games had made him really good and here we were teasing him. We all went to his game that week to see him play. We sat next to his mother and his sister, who never missed a game. And we all watched as Packy, the toughest kid we knew, stood on the sidelines. With two minutes to play, the coach put him in. His team was down by thirty, and it was clear it no longer mattered who was in the game. Afterwards, we kidded him and he made excuses, about the coach, about the weather, about everything. He only showed up to the bus stop with taped fingers once more after that, and we teased him so much he never did it again.

Packy did stick with football every season and after a couple of years he even played. But by that time a bunch of guys from the neighborhood had started playing, too, so it wasn't a big deal. The rest of the time Packy hung around with us. He never spent much time at his house. Packy's mom started working more and his dad spent more and more time on the porch, so Packy hardly ever went home. Even when it was time for dinner, he followed one of us guys home most nights. He was polite to our parents, so they always invited him to stay. My mom would even cook his favorites especially for him.

"Packy's got such good manners," she'd say. "I wish all of your friends were like him. Lord knows what would happen if all of you boys acted like Ronald."

"Aw mom," is all I would answer.

Packy was just one of the gang, a part of the neighborhood. Without him, it wouldn't be the same. He had his place. We needed him the same way we needed Ronny, or V, or even stupid Chad to push around, and we all accepted each other. That's what was so terrible about his leaving: we didn't think anyone would ever fill his spot.

When Packy came out the morning he was leaving, no one knew what to say. He stared at all of us, his friends, and we stared back. Finally, it was Ronny who had to say something.

"So...where exactly are you moving to?"

"We're moving to...um...Washington D.C. Yeah, that's right. Washington D.C."

"Howcum you're going there? And why do you have to go so soon? I mean, why didn't you tell us sooner?"

"I just found out myself. It's all been kept real quiet."

"Well, why didn't anyone tell you?"

"It's because...my dad...got a promotion. Yeah, it's a government job. We just found out. They said come right away. He left yesterday. I shouldn't be telling you this, but my dad is in the CIA."

"Your dad? Is in the CIA? Since when?"

"Since forever. But he got promoted, so I have to leave. We might be back though; at least that's what my mom says. These things aren't always permanent."

"School's gonna start in a few weeks. Aren't you gonna miss it?" V asked.

"My mom said it'd be better to start school there and then see what happens. I'll write you guys when I know for sure."

"But Packy," I said, "it's only four months until I can get my driver's permit. We had plans to…"

"Packy! It's time to go! Say goodbye," his mom called.

"Well, I gotta go. I'll miss you guys. You're the best friends I ever had."

I don't think one of us didn't want to cry, and if anyone had started, we all would have been bawling like a bunch of wimps.

"Goodbye Packy. Let us know when you're coming back."

"I will."

Then he did something I didn't expect. He shook all of our hands the way my favorite uncle did when I saw him once a year. It wasn't hello or goodbye, but it said everything at once and made you feel good inside, almost proud even though you hadn't done anything at all. Packy climbed up into the U-Haul and waved. We all stood in the street and watched it drive out of sight.

The next few days were a tough adjustment. We kept having an odd number of guys to make teams, and no one wanted to sit out, not even Chad. Spud wasn't the same. Baseball, football, and even swimming weren't the same. Then, after about three weeks, just before school was going to start, we were on our bikes riding to get ice cream because it was ninety degrees out and that's the best thing to do in the summer when it gets that hot, and we passed Packy's house. There was a car in the driveway and sitting on the front porch drinking a beer was Packy's dad. We couldn't believe it. Packy came home after all.

None of us had ever said more than hi to Mr. O'Leary,

but we rushed up to him like he was our best friend. "Hello Mr. O'Leary! How was Washington? Is Packy here?"

"Packy? He's with his mother," he said, popping another beer. "I ain't never been to Washington, neither. What are you talking about?"

"It's because Packy said…," and I stopped. "Is Packy going to come back here?"

"I don't know about that. He's…you kids…hey, get on outta here and quit bothering me. Packy doesn't live here anymore."

I watched as he raised the beer to his lips, watched beer dribble down his chin, and onto his sweat soaked t-shirt.

"Sorry," I said, and we all retreated off the porch to go get ice cream.

We would see Mr. O'Leary sitting on his porch every day, but we never stopped to talk to him again. A new family moved to the street two days before school started, one kid our age and an older, but not so good-looking, sister, and we made him block whenever we played football. He wasn't too bad, but he had a lot to learn.

The January after Packy left, Ronny got a letter addressed to all of us. It said:

> Dear Guys,
>
> I hope you are all doing great. I'm pretty good. I played football here this year. Coach says I'll start next year for sure, if I'm here. My mom says we might move back, to take care of my grandmother. We'll have to see. We went to the state championships but got beat 21-10. I scored a touchdown

on a fumble. Next year we're sure to win it all. I made a lot of new friends but none of them are as good as you guys. I got a girlfriend here, and she wears my jersey before every game. Hope you are all just as lucky. I'll write as soon as I know if we're coming back and send you a picture of my girlfriend. My girlfriend just showed up and she wants me to go out with her so I got to go.

Your Friend,
Packy

We wanted to write back, but there wasn't a return address. The postmark said New Jersey.

PALMER AVE.

The bridge over Main Street was the natural boundary between our neighborhood and the next one. It was, of course, an unspoken rule, but everyone obeyed it. It's true you might pass through to get somewhere, but you didn't stop just to hang out. It helped maintain the natural order of things. Although we rode the same bus as other kids, our bus dropped kids off in three distinct neighborhoods. Even in the summertime, we normally only played in our neighborhood. It doesn't make much sense to me now, because I was friends with lots of kids in school who would have been great to hang out with and they only lived a half a mile away, an easy bike ride or walk. But outside of school, we didn't socialize, except maybe at some party or big special event, until we were in high school. In high school, people could drive, and were in more organized team sports together, and were dating girls on the other end of town. But in junior high, we all rode the bus home, got off at our stop, and hung out with the same guys every day. Everyone seemed content with the arrangement and life went on as normal, until the day I got off the bus, walked back under the bridge, and stood, face to face, with the one kid I hated more than anyone else, on the corner of Palmer Ave.

Joey Zolkas was an idiot. He was also a bully. His specialty was picking on kids about two years younger than him and taunting them until he made them cry. This brought him immense satisfaction that I could not understand. And still, kids were drawn to him. Or forced to serve him. He was the one person I could point to and honestly say had no friends. The kids he was with were his cronies or stoolies, but not his friends. The kids, and there were only a few, were basically forced together because of the geographic location of their homes. Palmer Ave. was the first street past the bridge. Joey Zolkas lived there and often hung out under the bridge, smoking a cigarette he'd stolen from his parents, and generally acting like a troll. He was the gatekeeper out of the neighborhood and no one went by him without a comment or nasty remark. His turf stretched to the four-lane parkway that intersected Main Street. Beyond that was another great neighborhood where the other third of our bus lived. But it was this in-between, this no-man's land between the parkway and Palmer Ave., which Joey controlled.

It was uncomfortable to pass by him under the bridge, hidden in the shadows, animal-like in the dark corners, waiting to pounce. If he saw the chance to knock a kid off his bike, he did it. If a girl passed by, he'd call out terrible things, things that would get my mouth washed out with soap in my house. If you went by and he wasn't there, you breathed a sigh of relief and hoped he would still not be there when you came back. Usually, we passed by in groups, on the way to get pizza. Unless he had all of his lackeys, he would be quiet when outnumbered. Sometimes he would just shout at one kid, whoever was the easiest target, ignoring everyone else.

"Don't let him get to you," I'd say to Ronny or V, "he's just a jerk."

"Yeah, that's easy for you to say," they'd tell me, "he doesn't say anything to you."

And they were right. He didn't say anything to me

because I was as big as him. There were also more of us from our neighborhood than there were from his and he knew we stuck together. I also never backed down from him and so he had tried only one time to intimidate me. I was riding down past the bridge to pick up something for my mom at the store and passed him with two of his minions. They were talking to each other but as I approached they got quiet. The only sound was my bike tires on the pavement, smooth and steady. As I went past him, probably right at the point he thought I wouldn't hear him, he said, "Fag." His two little followers chuckled, stifling their laughter, although it no doubt thrilled them to see someone who wasn't them, get picked on.

I swung my bike around, pedaled hard, jumped the curb, and stopped fast in front of them. The two smaller kids ran. I stared Joey Zolkas in the face. "What did you say to me?"

"I didn't say nothing," he said, refusing to make eye contact and obviously furious that he had been abandoned and now stood here all alone. He started to walk away, no doubt to chase down his friends and beat the crap out of them.

"That's what I thought," I called after him. He wasn't there when I rode by a little later.

We didn't speak again until I came back to school after I was sick for a week with tonsillitis in the early spring of eighth grade. A week is a long time to be gone. It's enough time to forget that someone is coming back, and enough time to get the courage to do something stupid. And that's exactly what Joey Zolkas did.

Actually, it was more than a week. I got sick on Thursday and went to the school nurse second period. She took my temperature, checked my throat, and called my mom to come get me. My mom took me to the doctor, who put me on penicillin, and then home to bed. I didn't ride the bus that Thursday or Friday, and then stayed home all of the next week. By the second Thursday, Joey made his power move. He was the biggest kid on the bus with no one to oppose him, so he began his reign of terror.

The descriptions of those two days were horrifying. There is something about a kid like Joey, some part of their make-up that allows them to be ultra-sneaky and devious without always getting caught. Granted, they do get caught and punished sometimes, but usually it is when they are younger so they learn how to avoid trouble later. It's scary how good these kinds of kids are at causing mayhem but avoiding trouble. They are always on the fringe in the aftermath, saying, "It wasn't me!" There is enough conviction in their plea and not enough evidence to convict them, so they get off. That was what happened for those two days on the bus. He tortured kids with cruel names and Charlie horses. He smacked kids for flinching. He pelted kids with all sorts of objects and walked off the bus Scott-free.

On Friday after school, he decided to make his biggest move of all. He crossed under the bridge after getting off the bus and went to Jason Devereux's house. He essentially forced him to be his friend. When Jason and Joey were little, they went to the same babysitter. Even into first and second grade they were friends, sort of. Then Jason's mom started to see that Joey was trouble and wouldn't let Jason play with him. Jason lived on the opposite side of the bridge, one street in, and closest to Joey. He made excuses for why he couldn't play. His mom and dad made excuses, too. As time went on, Joey faded away, keeping to his own street, except for the occasional remark on the bus or when he was passed on the street. His reputation got worse, with rumors of him stealing things, shoplifting, and being a general all around juvenile delinquent. People said he stayed out of jail only because his father was a retired police officer who got him out of trouble. People also said his mother was a drunk. Their screaming matches were the stuff of legends on the street.

There was a stickball game going on in the street when Joey came up. He stole the ball and said he was playing. No one wanted to say anything.

"I think I have to go now," V said. "I have to babysit my brother." V left, but he was the only one who got to go.

"Good," Joey said. "Now we have even teams again. I'll pitch."

The guys said it was the longest game ever. Joey changed the rules as he went. He argued every call. He called everyone names, even his teammates, and he could never be out. When it got to be dinnertime and kids could leave, he followed Jason home.

"What are we doing tomorrow?" he asked Jason.

"Ummm...I think I'm going somewhere with my parents," he answered.

"Don't lie to me! You don't have nothing to do! I'll be over in the morning. Be ready to do something or else," he ordered.

On Saturday, Joey showed up. Jason's mom was shocked

to see him. She started to tell him Jason was busy, but then Jason came out and left with him. Jason had no choice. He knew Joey's "Or else" was not optional. He was scared but didn't want his parents to know. Later in the afternoon they met up with the guys again. Joey dominated them and chose all the games. When everyone left for dinner again, Joey told Jason, "I'll see you tomorrow."

"I have church in the morning," Jason said. "Then we go to my grandmother's for lunch. Then I have homework. There's a big project due for science. I probably won't be around tomorrow."

Joey was steamed. He liked his new power and didn't want it to end. He bossed everyone around and they listened to him, too. Plus, they weren't like the dweebs he usually hung around with. He decided he liked doing stuff, especially when he always won. "All right," he said, "but Monday we're hanging out. You'd better get your homework done." Then he headed back to his bridge to brood.

On Sunday Jason did go to church and to his grandmother's for lunch, but there was no science project due. He felt pretty proud of himself for tricking Joey. He was having a great time playing football with the guys in Ronny's yard when Joey showed up.

"I thought you had science to do?" he half-asked, half-accused Jason.

"Joey!" Jason was startled and nervous. "I…I…I…did. I did it already."

"Well, why didn't you call me?" Joey asked.

"I don't know," Jason answered.

"You do so know. You didn't want me around because

I'm better than all these punks at everything. Well guess what? I'm here now so it's time to pay up!"

"Pay up? Pay up what?" Jason asked and Joey punched him in the eye.

Jason went down, covering his eye and yelling, "Stop! Stop!" Joey Zolkas showed no mercy. He was on top of him, punching him in the head, the body, the arms as Jason tried to cover up. The other guys tried to pull Joey off of him, but he pushed them down, kicked Mark and Chad, and slapped, not punched but slapped, Ronny across the face. When his fury was spent, he said, "I'll see you tomorrow. Don't make me do this again," and he left.

The guys were embarrassed as much as hurt, except Jason, who was really hurt. He went home crying, or as it was described to me, sobbing, but the way a little kid does when they get in trouble. His parents called Joey's house, but the response was simple. It started with, "Boys will be boys," progressed to "They need to work it out themselves," and ended with "If your kid wasn't such a weakling, he wouldn't have gotten beat up!"

The Devereuxs were not pleased. Their advice to Jason was to stay away from Joey. If he came around, then come in the house. If he started something at school, tell a teacher. These are things all parents tell their children. None of these things was going to solve the problem.

Monday morning at the bus stop was something to see. It was like the walking wounded had arrived from a MASH unit. Everyone was beat up and bruised. That's when I heard the stories of the last week up until yesterday. My grandfather would say things like, "That really makes my blood boil!" but I didn't know what that meant until right at that moment. Jason Devereux was my friend. He had always been long and skinny, more like a deer than a boy, not fragile and weak, but certainly no fighter. But he was easy to like and get along with. He followed, but he was a peacemaker, and when he spoke up, it was because what he had to say was important. He had been there through most of my neighborhood adventures, from nearly killing his cousin from Kansas sledding, to illegally catching the biggest fish we had ever seen. He always tempered my recklessness by trying to talk some sense into me, and I figured he probably saved me from sure death more than once. Joey Zolkas had a reckoning coming. I owed my friend that much.

Jason didn't show up for the bus that morning and neither did Joey. It turns out both of their parents thought it better to drop them off for school. That means I had to wait, too, but not for long. In first period math I sat next to Jason and when I saw his face I was shocked. He had two great big raccoon eyes and a bruise on his cheek. He had more bruises on his arms. He looked really beat up. It surprised our math teacher enough that she called him out in the hallway to ask if he was okay and if there were problems at home. His mom also got a phone call at home. She explained everything and the school promised to watch out for him, to keep the boys apart. This was also not going to solve the problem.

My stomach was in knots all day. I knew exactly how to solve the problem. It was just a matter of time, until the end of the day. It didn't take a genius to know that fighting in school was a bad idea. First, you'd get suspended. Then, you'd face your father. The school suspension would be nothing compared to my father. My parents were against fighting. Yes, my dad would say, you can defend yourself. No, you can't go around fighting. This paradox was more than I could handle. It was a very good thing that I had my cousins to help me clear this up. That, and my grandfather, who taught us boys a few things because, as he said, we couldn't grow up a bunch of wimps.

When I got on the bus that afternoon Joey Zolkas was already in the back beating some kid up with his own fist. "Why you hittin' yourself? Why you hittin' yourself? Why you hittin' yourself?" he said.

"Hey!" I said, "Let that kid go."

He turned to face me, still holding the kid's wrist. Tears were welling up in the little kids eyes, probably from pain, shame, and the hope of being released all rolled together.

"Who's gonna make me?" Joey said.

"I am."

"You wanna make something of it?"

"Yep. I do."

Joey let the kid go and he scampered towards the front of the bus, wincing and rubbing his wrist. The bus was full and ready to leave the school. Our very old and possibly legally blind bus driver who never noticed anything, like Joey slapping a kid around in the back of the bus, saw us standing in the aisle.

"You kids sit down back there!" he hollered.

Neither of us wanted to flinch. "Is this about your girlfriend?" he said, pointing to Jason sitting just two seats away. I realized everyone on the bus was looking at us, waiting for something to happen.

"Shut your fat mouth Zolkas. He's not my girlfriend, he's my friend. If you ever had a friend, you might understand that. But you're just a punk who needs an attitude adjustment. I'll make you cry like a baby when I finish with you."

"You don't scare me, you queer bait! I'm gonna smash your face in!"

"You're the queer. I'm no little kid. Do you like picking on little boys and girls? Does it make you feel tough? Are you a big man for beating up guys half your size? It's time to pick on somebody your own size. And I'm going to beat the crap out of you."

"Sit down back there!" the bus driver yelled again. "I swear I'll pull this bus over!"

"Let's do it then," Joey said, "name the time and place," but he wasn't confident. In fact, he was scared. It was in his face, in the eyes. He wanted to talk tough, but he knew I wasn't going to lie down on the ground and let him beat me. He wanted to look strong in front of his underling friends, but underneath he was shaking.

"As soon as I get off the bus, I'll meet you at Palmer Ave. I want to whip you on your own street so later you don't cry like a girl and say I had an advantage."

"I'll fight you right now!"

"That's because you're stupid. I'm not getting kicked out of school. You may be too dumb to care, but you can wait five minutes for your beating." Then I sat down next to Ronny. Joey retreated into his seat and started punching the back of it. He was working himself into a frenzy, frothing and spitting and cussing. What he didn't know was that I was terrified. I hadn't been in a real fist fight in at least two years. Once you build your reputation, you can live on it for a long time. I was a tough kid who didn't take crap, but I also wasn't a jerk. I stuck up for the little guy, but it earned respect. Now, I had to go through with this. I didn't want to, but I had to.

At Joey's stop he brushed by me, trying to give me a shove. I shoved back and said, "See you soon." Joey was still in a rage, his face beat red. The bus had never been so quiet as when he walked off. When the doors closed, it erupted, kids asking me if I was really going to fight him. Even our bus driver knew something was up, although he didn't know what, as he tried to get everyone to sit down again. At my stop, I got off followed by all of my friends. The kids still on the bus rushed to the windows facing us to get a final look.

"You don't have to fight him, you know," Jason said to me. This made me laugh a little because he was looking out for me. "But," he continued, "I'm not going to stop you either."

We started up the street like something out of a western. It was high noon, showdown time. This had been building for a long time and had to be settled today. Ahead, I could see kids running from their bus stops down towards the bridge. Behind me, I could hear kids coming from their stops, racing to get there before the fight started.

As I got closer, there was Joey Zolkas throwing his jean jacket on the ground and dancing around like he was loosening up. I handed my books to V and my jacket to Jason as I walked under the bridge to the corner of Palmer Ave.

In movies, people always go over ground rules before

a fight and talk about what they are going to do or what happens when somebody wins, like what they get for a prize or trophy or something. But in real life it doesn't happen that way. Joey Zolkas had been embarrassed and he was pissed. The talking had already happened on the bus. I also figure Joey must have known there would be some retribution for beating up a bunch of my friends and had thought about this fight for awhile. As soon as I got close, he let out a scream and charged me, swinging wildly and hitting me in the chest and arms three or four times before I got my hands up to protect my face.

He hit incredibly hard, and was still slobbering and cussing. His first rush surprised me, but now I had my feet under me and jabbed back, popping him in his nose, over and over. I didn't think he felt it until there was blood on my knuckles and he backed off to regroup. I moved around, now very aware that a huge group of kids was watching, screaming, cheering, and mostly calling for me to knock his block off. He came again in a second rush, even more frantic than before, swinging, missing, swinging, hitting, while I dodged and ducked, trying to counter punch. I could hear my grandfather's words: Keep your balance, block, and look for an opening. He'll tire out before you and then you've got him.

My left eye was swollen and my ribs hurt, but he was wearing down fast. We were both bloodied up pretty good, but I was just getting ready to attack. I unloaded a big right to his cheek and he made a weird whining noise which let me know it hurt. Then I went to work on his body. I wanted his ribs to hurt at much as mine, as much as Jason Devereux's face, as much as that kid's wrist on the back of the bus. I punched and punched for every kid he had ever tortured, until he fell down, clutching his ribs, and just for a second, I thought he was starting to cry.

I felt nothing, no pain, no joy, no hate. I was numb except for the thought to finish him when he made his last stand. I knew he would, too. He was no "punch him once and he'll run away" bully. He was strong and determined, knowing his entire reputation as a tough guy hung in the balance. He got to his feet, pure hatred in his stare, and came at me.

Another thing my grandfather taught us boys was that no man is more dangerous than at the end. At the time, it sounded like war stories, but experiencing it, it was true. But Joey Zolkas didn't come at my face or my gut this time. He went for my legs. He wanted to get me down, get on top, and pummel me. It was his M.O. I sidestepped his rush and kneed him in the face, leaving his blood on my jeans and Joey in a heap on the ground. I got on top of him, like I was going to pound him into the dirt, and he covered his face with his arms and started to cry.

"No more," he sobbed, "you win. No more. Please... please..."

Around me kids were chanting, "Kill him! Kill him!" I looked at him, at what I had done to him, and it was enough.

"Don't you ever come into my neighborhood again," I told him. "And if you ever touch my friends or any little kid while I'm around, I'll bust you worse than this. Swear it!"

"I swear," he said, and then I told his lackeys to pick him up.

That was the last real fight I was ever in. Sure, in high

school there were a few pushing matches and some hot tempers during basketball or hockey. But nothing like this. Reputation is everything and mine was permanently linked with the beat down of Joey Zolkas. Something like that goes a long way to keeping you out of future fights.

I knew I was going to be in trouble with my father. I figured I would be grounded for a week, maybe two. Standard punishment was no T.V. but it was okay. I did what I thought was right for my friends and for myself. Sometimes, you have to take a stand.

As for Joey Zolkas, he was still a jerk. At least he didn't bother kids as much, and never when I was around. I always had the feeling he'd come at me from behind, so I didn't turn my back on him. From then on, I'd just stare him down and he'd back off from whatever kid he'd started with. By the time we entered high school, he'd started smoking pot and getting into new kinds of trouble. He was arrested a couple of times, and then he dropped out. Eventually, he wasn't under the bridge anymore or on Palmer Ave. at all. I honestly don't know what happened to him after that, but in my mind I see him as a volunteer sheriff in some podunk rural town, pulling his gun out at routine traffic stops and harassing the locals.

That night, when my father came home from work, he got two phone calls. The first was from the Devereuxs. They wanted to tell my father to go easy on me. The next one was from Joey Zolkas' mom. She wanted to let my father know how her innocent son had been beaten up by his bully son. "Boys will be boys," my father said, "they need to work it out themselves," and he hung up the phone.

LUCKY BREAK

jumped straight up, reaching as high as I could above my head, and stabbed the ball out of the air. I had been watching this fool throw low, lazy passes for three quarters, and now it was going to cost him. Juking right, I went to my left with a quick cross-over dribble and went straight for the basket. The point guard had different ideas, running hard to catch me and staying right on my heels as I went up under the basket. We were both going hard, so when I left my feet he couldn't stop and he ran right through me.

The next couple of minutes are still foggy. I remember thinking, "I'm going into the bleachers," but I was really still calm gliding through the air. As I came down, my left leg went between the risers and slammed me down. The point guard went face first into the first row. I almost landed on top of him and probably would have, had my leg not been caught. I hit the back of my head hard, felt sort of dizzy, and started to black out.

I was brought back by the sound of my coach, Mr. Trolley, screaming at me to get up. It was like in the *Rocky* movies when Mick is yelling at Rocky to get up off the canvas, only I was partially inverted and stuck. I rolled my head and looked at the point guard. His nose was bleeding badly; he'd broken it and would end up with two black eyes the next day, but he was lucky. I knew I had to get back up, because as my team mates always joked, the trolley was coming to get me. I pulled my leg out from the bleachers, turned, and tried to stand. I immediately fell down onto the gym floor. The adrenaline was pumping so hard I hadn't noticed the watermelon-sized purple mass swelling on my leg. I also hadn't noticed the blood running down the back of my head until I ran my hand through my hair to wipe the sweat out of my face. Then the wooziness came back and I lay down on the glossy polyurethane gym floor and stared up at the popcorn ceiling. There was a thumping in my ears, drowning out all other sounds. It was one of the weirdest feelings seeing people scrambling around, talking, yelling, calling for help, but I didn't hear any of it. I only heard the repetitive thump-thump that was the throbbing of my leg.

"Jesus, look at that," Trolley said. "Well, kid, your leg is busted. Let's get you to the nurse." He yelled to two of my team mates who helped me up and walked me out the back of the gym hopping on one leg. Ol' Trolley was one tough bird. He wanted the floor cleared so the team could finish the game. He also wanted me to stop bleeding on his court. The nurse's office was back here and as much as I wanted to lie down, I made the guys stop at the water fountain and hold me up while I drank. I had the worst thirst of my life come over me and I drank and drank. Then we went into the nurse's office where she went into hysterics.

"What happened? Oh my God! Is your leg broken? Why did Coach Trolley move you?" she asked.

I stared at her for a second, and then said, "Can I lie down?"

A minute later, Coach Trolley came in. "Good hustle out there, today." Then, looking down at my leg, he said, "That's a tough break, kid. You were having a good season."

And he was right, it was a tough break. In fact, it was two breaks. My leg had snapped clean in half, breaking my tibia and my fibula. The next half hour was painful, and not just physically. Vice Principal Chalmers came in and tried to cheer me up with his corny jokes. "Trying to get the girls to notice you, huh? You'll get all the sympathy now," he said. In reality, he was probably more concerned about the school getting sued or something.

I watched as they cleaned up the other kid, the one who took me out. They packed his nose with gauze and drove him to the hospital to get checked out. He sounded kind of funny when he said, "No har feelin, white?" and shook my hand, but I was still ticked off that he had just ended my J.V. basketball career. I was still fuming when the ambulance arrived to take me to the emergency room. My mood quickly changed when the ambulance EMTs showed up. They were hilarious. I think it's because they were so used to working with dead people, so when they had a live teenager, they had some fun.

"All right, man, what do we have? Ooohh, nasty looking leg. Let's get it stabilized!" He took out what looked like a pizza box and formed it to fit my leg.

"What's that?" I asked. "Don't I get an air cast?" All the athletes on T.V. got air casts and carted off in style. I had already gotten dragged off the court and down a hallway. I should at least get an air cast.

"An air cast? I thought this was a junior high? Did you just sign with the NBA? Gary, you hear Mr. NBA? He wants an air cast!"

"I heard him, Daryl. Sorry kid, you get the pizza box. You want Brooklyn or Chicago style?"

I was disappointed, but I had to laugh. These guys were funny. They loaded me up on the gurney and into the back of the ambulance, the whole time telling me about all of their sports injuries. Every time Gary said something, Daryl one-upped him. The school nurse couldn't get a word in, but she finally managed to tell me she had talked to my parents and they would meet me at the hospital.

As we started down the road I asked, "Aren't you going to turn on the lights and the sirens?" Every ambulance in every movie or T.V. show I had ever seen had lights and sirens blaring. I felt I was missing the experience.

"Daryl, the NBA All-Star wants lights and sirens? What do you say?"

"You know we don't do that unless it's an emergency."

"C'mon," I said. "What's fun about an ambulance unless you can speed and run red lights?"

They both laughed. "Hang on back there," Daryl said, and he took off, sirens screaming.

At the hospital, it was crazy. There were more patients than places to put them. I was put in a hallway and left to wait with half a dozen other patients. They said they'd look at me when my parents arrived and signed the paperwork.

"Can I have an aspirin or something?" I asked.

"Not until your parents fill out the forms," the orderly told me.

Daryl and Gary were cool. They hung out and kept telling me stories. They could have just dumped me and left, but they said it was fine, they'd wait for my mom and dad to show up. That took awhile, mostly because of the school nurse. She told them the wrong hospital.

"We were going crazy, I was so worried," my mom said. "We looked all over for you and no one knew where you were. Finally, we got a hold of Mr. Chalmers and he told us where they sent you."

"We still don't know how this happened. You have to tell us," my dad said.

"Hey, we're taking off," Gary said. "You'll be okay, kid. Watch out for those bleachers – they'll get you every time!"

"See you. Thanks guys. Best ambulance ride ever," I said.

My mom went and got all of the paperwork and filled it out while I told the whole story to my dad. "So, did it go in?" he asked.

"Did what go in?"

"The shot. Did you hit it before the kid hit you?" That was my dad. I'm dying here but he wants to know if the basket counted.

"I don't know, dad. I didn't see it. I was in the stands!" He thought that was funny, but the longer I waited for pain medication, the less funny it was to me. When my mom came back I had to re-tell the entire story. I was getting irritable.

When the nurse finally checked on me an hour later, it wasn't to give me anything. It was to tell me I couldn't have anything until after they did x-rays to see if I needed surgery. It still took twenty minutes before they wheeled me into x-ray. When they finished I was told the doctor would be with me shortly. I was wheeled into another room, sectioned off by curtains, to wait. Another hour went by. I thought I was a tough kid, but it was getting close to five hours. I was still in my stinky uniform, with my leg in a pizza box. I wasn't allowed to eat or drink, but that didn't matter because all I wanted was drugs.

The room was small and hot. Patients were on both walls, our feet pointing at each other, maybe two feet away, separated by a small aisle so nurses could get to all of us. I was really getting upset. No one would help. Everyone said the same thing: The hospital is understaffed and overcrowded. If it wasn't an emergency, we needed to be patient. I started to think of *Gone with the Wind*, which was my mother's favorite movie, and although I would never admit it, I kind of liked it and had watched it at least ten times with her. There's a scene where everybody is shot up and dying so they are lying in the hot sun, covered in flies and stench. I started thinking how the one doctor couldn't handle everything and he had to go home and sleep. Then I wondered if that was happening here. Were all the doctors home asleep? I felt like I was dying and I sure did stink, so all I needed was the flies and I'd be a goner.

A new nurse came in to check on us, the non-emergency, walking wounded rejects, stuck in a back closet waiting, and waiting, and waiting. I was closest to the door so she asked me first, "Can I get you anything?"

"A doctor, and some drugs. I'm dying here," I told her. She clearly didn't believe me. So my mother added, "He's been here seven hours. Can't he have something for the pain?"

"Oh!" she said. "Does anyone else know he's been waiting so long? Has he seen the doctor yet?"

"No, he's had x-rays, but no doctor has checked on him yet," my mom said.

"I'll check on the doctor right away," she said and started to turn and walk out.

"Nurse, help me," the old man across the aisle said. "I'm not supposed to be here!"

She stopped and turned to check the old man. As I said, the aisle was not wide. And the nurse was not small. She was the biggest nurse I had ever seen, and I don't mean tall. She was wide and when she spun around her big rear end rammed right into my elevated foot. I let out a yelp like a dog that has gotten underfoot and stepped on.

"Oh! I'm so sorry! I'm so sorry!" she kept saying.

"Please just get the doctor," my mother said.

One minute later the doctor appeared holding my x-rays. "Hmmm….," he said, holding them up to the light. "Looks like a good clean break. We won't cast it tonight, it's too swollen. I'll check it again tomorrow morning. If the swelling goes down, I'll cast it then. Get some rest. I'll have you sent up to a room."

"Doc," I said, "can I have some drugs?"

He looked at my chart. "Oh, you've been here awhile, huh? I'll make sure the nurse gives you something before they move you. See you in the morning." He left and the nurse came back a minute later with the biggest needle ever made. I think it was for sedating elephants.

"Where do you want it?" she asked.

I tilted up on my side and pulled my shorts down enough to show her one cheek. There was a sharp pain and then relief.

* * * * *

When I woke up in the morning, I had no idea where I was. It looked like a little girl's room, all bright yellow and pink. Big Bird was painted on the wall in front of me. He was playing with some Muppet I didn't know. Then it dawned on me, I was in the hospital. A nurse came in to take my temperature.

"Where am I?" I asked her.

"You're in the pediatric wing at the hospital. There were no more beds upstairs, so they put you in here last night. You slept the whole night."

"Have you seen my parents?"

"They left late last night. They said they would be back this morning after they got your sisters to school. They came last night, too, but you slept through their visit. This morning we're going down to x-rays and then to the casting room if everything looks good. The doctor is already here."

She called another nurse and they transferred me to a gurney, then pushed me down to the x-ray room. I waited there until the doctor came and looked at the film.

"Hmmm...looks good," Dr. Pierce said. "We won't need to operate. We can set the bone and cast you up. You'll need a hip cast. I need both of these bones to stay immobilized so they knit together. They'll be stronger than ever when you heal." Then he turned to the nurse who had brought me down and said, "Come with me."

On the way to the casting room I asked Dr. Pierce about himself. He was friendly and told me how he had served twenty years as an Army surgeon before going into private practice. I should have known this did not bode well for what came next.

"Nurse, you'll assist me in setting this leg and casting it," he told her.

The pediatric nurse, clearly taken aback, said, "I've never done that. I work with the babies on the pediatric floor!"

"Nonsense," he told her, "you're a trained nurse. Just do exactly what I tell you." There was no arguing with him. Then he turned to me. "Okay, swing your legs over the side of the gurney."

"What?

"Your legs. Swing them over the side of the gurney so I can cast your leg."

"But my leg is broken. I can't…"

"You can and you will. If you want to get out of this hospital, you need to start doing things for yourself."

I looked at the nurse, but she looked like she was in shock. I gave a grunt and, using both hands, lifted my broken leg over the side as I sat up and let my legs dangle. It was painful. I was starting to sweat. The doctor held the x-rays up to examine them.

"Nurse, hold the gurney." He looked me in the eye and said hold tight, this will hurt. He felt where the bones in my leg were broken, grabbed both the upper and lower halves of my leg, and popped the bones back together.

I gritted my teeth and let out an ugh sound, fighting back the tears and the pain. I swear the pediatric nurse almost fainted. My fingers were white from gripping the gurney so tightly.

"Good," Dr. Pierce said, "now breathe. That's what I want to see, pure grit. You did fine. Don't move. Nurse, get me…"

I don't know what he said next. The blood was thumping in my ears again. He was ordering the nurse to get things, and together they started casting my leg all the way to my hip. It felt so heavy and wet, like someone pulling my ankle to the floor. The cast was still drying when Dr Pierce said, "Now put your legs back on the gurney."

I was determined now that this man would not be able to make me give in and ask for help. I would show him John Wayne toughness if that was what it took to go home. Sweat poured down my face as I lifted my broken leg back on the gurney, and relief swept over me as I lay back down.

"Nurse, make sure that leg is elevated. Minimum movement until tomorrow. I don't want that leg swelling in the cast. I'll be in tomorrow morning to check him. His family doctor will be by this afternoon. Good job, son. You showed some grit today."

The doctor left and the nurse started to cry. I was embarrassed. I didn't know what to say. "It's okay," I finally said. "It's over now."

"That was so horrible. Are you okay? What can I get for you?"

"Could you get me some pain killers?" I asked. And she did.

That night my family all showed up to visit. The adults went down for coffee, leaving my cousins, Matt and Mike to look out for me. They put gum on my big toe. They ate all of my candy that my aunt brought me. There was no mercy. Piranhas smell blood in the water and feast. I was exhausted when they left.

The doctor said everything was going fine, so after two

more days in the hospital and some physical therapy to prove I could get up and down stairs on crutches, they let me go home. The first week was sweet. Everyone waited on me and let me watch whatever I wanted on T.V. Friends came to visit and brought me "Get Well Soon!" cards. It was too good to last and that's when my mother informed me that my teachers were coming to tutor me at home after school, starting Monday. Since Dr. Pierce wanted me home to recuperate for a month, it meant three weeks of having my teachers come to my house. It was okay except some of them were really boring and my mother would keep them talking and drinking tea long after they should have left. It's like they had no social lives or something. When the month was up, I went to see Dr. Pierce. He said my leg was healing like he wanted. He cut the hip cast off and put on a shorter one. Man, was my leg gross, all covered in dead skin and withering away. At least now I could move my knee, so that made me happy. He also told me it was time to go back to school. My cast was to stay on for two more months and I needed to be careful, but I'd get to see my friends again. The doctor was worried that because it was the middle of winter, I might fall. That's why he wanted to talk to mother alone for a few minutes. On the car ride home my mother told me the bad news: I couldn't take my regular bus to school because it was a long walk to the bus stop. Instead, I would be getting picked up a half an hour before I normally would – by the short bus.

* * * * *

The first morning was brutal – dark, cold, and early. I had been allowed to sleep in every day since coming home from the hospital, so this early morning wake-up was a lousy way to start back. I won't lie either, I was nervous. As kids you always joked about someone getting on the short bus because they were stupid or retarded or something. I know how terrible that sounds, but it's the way we talked and what we said. Ignorance is no excuse, but that would quickly change. Now, I was about to become one of them.

The bus pulled up and my Dad helped me out the door the first day. He didn't want me slipping in the snow. When he saw me get on board, he waved goodbye and I was on my own. I was surprised to find the bus empty. Apparently, I was the first stop. The bus driver was an old guy in a baseball hat that said *Florida! The Good Life!* across the front.

"Good morning! My name's Ray. Welcome to my bus. Sit anywhere you want...except the two seats directly behind me...and the other front seat. Those are reserved for my usual guests."

Another two rows of seats had been removed for wheelchair seating and a ramp to get on the bus. That left me three choices. I took one of the back seats and settled in.

"You're the first stop," Ray said from the front. "It takes us almost 45 minutes to get to school with our route, so if you want, you can take a nap. I don't mind."

"Thanks," and I dozed off.

When we got to school I yawned and stretched and looked around. There were a bunch of kids I had never seen staring at me. They quickly turned back around, embarrassed at being caught, and then we started to get off the bus. There was a kid in a wheelchair waiting for Ray to put the ramp down. "Hey," he said, "you snore loud." He laughed and now I was embarrassed.

"Thanks for the heads up," I said as I got off the bus.

"I'll meet you here at 3:00p.m.," Ray said.

"Great," I thought. "I get picked up early to get here and late to go home." I went in the back of the school with the rest of the kids and started my day.

School wasn't bad. I got lots of welcome back well wishes. I was allowed to leave class early and bring a friend to carry my books. I could show up late and teachers never said anything or if they did I could tell them the halls were crowded and I had to wait. At the end of the day I went to the back of the school, the same doors I went out of in an ambulance a month before, and waited for Ray. While waiting, I attempted to comfort myself by reasoning that it would only be for a few weeks and then things would be back to normal. I didn't want to be bothered with anyone, so I would just keep to myself until this whole thing was over. But things don't always work out like we plan, and for that I am grateful.

Ray let me sulk for two days, probably to get it out of my system, and then he decided it was time to have a talk. He started slow, talking about me, what I was like and what I liked. I was too young to realize where he was going until it was already happening as he showed me how similar I was to the kids I rode with each day but never spoke to other than a hello. He knew what I was thinking, that I wouldn't be on this bus forever and that I couldn't wait to be gone. But these kids were staying. Their problems didn't end when the doctors took the cast off, but they still didn't act miserable, like me. I was embarrassed because I knew it was all true. That's when I really started to listen.

Being thankful for what I have, not bitter for what I couldn't have, hadn't occurred to me. He talked about each student I rode with on the bus, because he knew each of them and wanted me to know them, too. Like Emily, who had been in therapy for almost three years but wasn't responding to any treatment. Despite this, she was always cheerful, always confident that she would walk on her own again one day. Or Scott, who not only thought I snored loud, but also played basketball and tennis, was in more school activities than I knew existed, and did more in the community than I ever thought of doing. He humanized them all, which is more than I could fully comprehend then, but what I would grow to appreciate as I adopted his style as an adult.

When he finished talking, I fought back the tears and resolved to start fresh the next day by greeting everyone as they got on the bus and having a conversation with each of them individually. The next few months flew by, and I was sad when it came to an end. I never passed a single one of them in the hallway again without saying hello, or stopping to chat, or to ask about Ray. The pain and embarrassment of that basketball game was far outweighed by what I felt that one day, in that one conversation with a bus driver in a ridiculous Florida hat. But what I discovered about myself, and what I learned about others, that was without question the luckiest break of all.

FISHING

SEE THE LIVE MERMAIDS! was painted in three foot tall letters on the sign outside the entrance to the Water Arena. *The Great Adventure* was not quite the "great" its name aspired to, but as far as amusement parks go, it was a good way to spend a summer day. There is a certain similarity between amusement parks that were built Post-World War II, usually in the craze of the 1950s baby boom, and this one was aging as gracefully as any of them that I had been to in my short life.

The park opened in mid-May, when the college kids came home, and closed the beginning of October, with fewer days and shorter hours starting in September, when the same college kids left again. It was a short season, but I don't remember a single summer when we didn't go at least a half a dozen times. It was almost like summer didn't start until the park opened for the year.

There was one good roller coaster, The Screamer, and one rickety, not-so-good one, The Rocket, which we always rode anyway. It was believed by every kid I knew that when you rode The Rocket, you faced death because that old coaster was bound to collapse in the middle of a ride, making the experience much scarier than it really was. But what a way to go, we all thought. The midway was standard fare, games and cotton candy, popcorn and hot dogs, and sometimes you went home with a stuffed tiger. The other rides were also good, and the owners always kept the place up. I never remember going there and finding a ride down for repair. It was a good place to go with your friends or to take a girl on a first date, and you would always run into people you knew so it was fun.

Although everyone had their favorite ride, the real attraction at *The Great Adventure* had always been its sideshows. It had one of the biggest collection of "freaks" at one time, and I vaguely remember seeing them when I was little. By the time I was a teenager, they were gone, no longer politically correct, and replaced with a variety of milder entertainment, like magic shows.

The one constant was the Water Arena, also known as the Aquadrome, a name I could never quite figure out. When my father was little, he told me stories of shows that featured dolphins and high divers, but they were also gone before I was born. In their place water ballets were born, reminding people of something from the black and white movies of the 1930s, featuring bathing beauties in swimsuits performing feats of wonder. The women were always gorgeous, moving through the water like they were born of the nymphs of the sea. They did three shows a day, which were always at capacity. Despite the fact that all of my friends complained how boring they were to watch, they still always wanted to go, and the complaints lessened considerably the older everyone got. It became less about the show and more about the performers for sure.

The highlight of the show, no question about it, was the mermaids. They were the most beautiful women I had ever seen. The costumes they wore were very revealing, especially to a teenage boy, covered in sequins, these amply endowed swimmers did not leave much to the imagination, as my grandmother would say, barely covered on top and squeezed into their fish tales on the bottom. They were full bodied, and needed to be to perform the way they did, breaking through the water from below, turning, flipping, and waving goodbye with their tails as they swam under water through a gate into an enormous tank in the tent adjoining the arena. After the show, you could pay to see the mermaids up close through the glass, a remnant of the true sideshow days, and the lines were always long.

One Sunday, my grandfather got the family together for a day at the park. There were picnic areas that families could use, for barbeques and some old fashioned fun. There were fireworks that night, which happened a dozen times at the park during the summer, so he thought it would be a great way to end a perfect summer day. We had a good time; the whole family was there. I especially liked being with my cousins, Matt and Mike, because they wanted to ride all the rides no one else would go on with me.

Late in the afternoon, after the last water show, Matt and Mike told me they had something crazy, unbelievable to show me. It's no secret they lived a bit more dangerously than most, so what they meant by that was anyone's guess. As the crowd filed out, we waited a couple minutes until we were the last ones in the Water Arena.

"Okay, we need to move quick," Matt said. He led us down and out a service entrance behind the fences that kept the public from seeing the maintenance workers or performers between shows. We moved quietly around the tent that adjoined the arena and came to a building where the performers prepared for the shows. Honestly, it looked more like a building from the zoo, and probably had been used to house animals at some point before it was converted to dressing rooms.

"Prop me up," Mike said to us, and pointed to a small vent window on the side of the building. Matt and I, each holding a foot, lifted him so he could peek through the window. "Sweet mother of mercy," Mike said softly, "they're in there!"

We dropped Mike, who was smiling as if he had just witnessed a miracle. "My turn, get me up there quick," Matt said. His response was the same as we let him down. I still had no idea what I was supposed to see, but they both said to hurry or I would miss it. They grabbed my feet and pushed me up into the air. Through that dirty window I saw the most beautiful sight I had ever seen--mermaids undressing.

Now, I understand how this sounds. It's easy to say that we were just some perverted Peeping Toms, hormonal teenagers, and to call us gross and disturbed. But what people forget is that this was before the internet; it wasn't that easy at our age to see what we were seeing. It took real effort and usually some sort of creepy guy at school you had to befriend just to get a peek at a magazine he stole from his step-dad. This was different though. This was real. It was actually happening and as far as I knew, it was a once in a lifetime experience. It was like a story out of Greek mythology, where a huntsman gazed upon Artemis bathing, or like catching a glimpse of a nymph frolicking in a woodland pool of water. I was mesmerized.

Everyone had their favorite mermaid from the show, and I was no different. I fixed my attention on the mermaid who I had always fantasized about, a very busty, chestnut haired goddess, who, as she undressed, caused the blood to rush into my face and my chest to ache from longing to be with her. Looking back, in a way it was a last moment of naïveté for me, and one, for a long time, I wished I could re-live. To me, as she pulled off her fish tale, I finally understood perfection. Her proportions were perfect, her curves exquisite. As she giggled and turned to talk to her companions, I saw for the first time her tattoo. It was a dolphin jumping free of the ocean, hidden from the world but revealed now to me, privately, as if we were sharing a secret together, my mermaid and I.

Now, today, I understand when people say, "So what? Everyone has tattoos," and dismiss this boyhood fantasy for just that. But this was really a big deal. Growing up, very few people I knew, or had ever seen, had tattoos. A few of my dad's friends who had been in the military had them, but it was usually one tattoo on their arm. A woman with a tattoo, this was almost scandalous, and simply added to the erotic nature of the entire scene. As I was memorizing every detail, every curve of her perfect body, determined to keep this vision of perfection with me as a rite of passage into manhood, my cousins dropped me. And they ran. So I ran after them.

Out of breath, the three of us stopped behind a dumpster, panting heavily, and I made a disgusted face at them as I breathed in the stench of garbage left out in the summer heat. A seagull pecked at the partially opened bag on top of the partially closed dumpster. When I could speak, I asked, "What was that?"

"What?"

"You freaking dropped me? And took off? Seriously?"

They both laughed. "We said someone's coming. You

just didn't hear us because you were seeing boobs for the first time. You went boob deaf," Matt said, and they both laughed.

"I..no I...," I tried to speak, but it was no use. So I grinned and laughed with them, and we high-fived, and shared details of what we had seen. Like the great Odysseus before us, we had come so close to the Sirens and had survived. It felt absolutely heroic, gazing on the forbidden and living to tell the tale.

For the rest of the afternoon and into the fireworks that night, I could only think of her, my tattooed mermaid. I hoped to see her walking through the park, hoped to approach her and tell her what a great performer she was, possibly the best I'd ever seen, but it didn't happen. For the rest of the summer, each time I visited the amusement park, I would make sure I caught her show. Each time I saw her, I fell in love again with a woman I would never know.

My grandfather, in addition to planning family get-togethers, was also a great fisherman. He would stop whatever he was doing if someone said, "Let's go fishing," and just go. He loved taking his grandkids more than anything else. He offered free lessons at the dock the next day when he out fished us, so there were lots of free lessons offered. That fall, after the amusement park had shut down for the season, and my mermaid had gone wherever mermaids go for the winter, my grandfather took me fishing in the river, down on the bank near the bridge.

"Who knows what we'll catch today? There's everything in this river," he said, and he meant it. Over the years he had caught more than 30 types of fish here, some of which had no business being in this river at all. As we fished together that cool autumn afternoon, I let my thoughts be carried by the current, down the river, into the ocean, deep into the sea. I was jerked to a start when my rod bent double, a heaviness I had never before felt, trying to pull me into the water, forcing me to cry out and pull back with all my might. As my grandfather rushed to help me, the tremendous swirl of a tail breached the water, slapped down, and dove, breaking my line. I was in complete shock.

"Grampa, what was that?" I asked.

"I don't know. I've never seen anything like it." Then he smiled and looked me in the face and said, "I think you just hooked a mermaid! Now you have a fish story to tell!"

I stared at him in utter disbelief, unable to fully understand what had just happened.

The following summer, she wasn't there. A copy of her was there, a chestnut haired, full bodied swimmer, but it wasn't her. She was gone, back to the sea to swim with the dolphins, to frolic with the nereids, to remain the unattainable object of perfection to a young man whom she did not know had gazed upon her beauty and been changed forever.

EGGS OVER HENDERSON

The backseat of the patrol car smelled less like puke and bum piss than I had expected. It smelled more like the disinfectant found in schools and hospitals. But then again, what did I know? They probably just hosed the backseat out every night. At least I wasn't in handcuffs, so that was something.

Just a few minutes before, I was being vehemently berated by a very intense officer who informed me how lucky I was that I was one block out of his jurisdiction.

"Believe me, boy, if you did this just up the street, you'd already be in lock-up. Punks like you that do stupid things need to be taught a lesson. And you'd be in general pop, not juvey, so you'd get a real taste for what life is like when you break the law."

He was intense. He went on his rant for more than five minutes until the officer who now had me in the back of his car showed up. I was genuinely concerned for my safety the whole time as he seemed to also be encouraging the group of college students who had been involved to press charges and prosecute to the fullest extent of the law.

Until Officer Finley showed up, I really thought I was done for. I had no idea what happened to my friends and no idea what to say to my parents when I had to call them from the station. What had started as a really boring Wednesday night just a few weeks before summer vacation had turned into an intense reality check. It's funny how a couple of hours can change your perspective.

Around 8 o'clock we were in Ronny's garage playing ping-pong. It was a pretty standard week night. Teenagers complaining how boring everything is and how there is never anything to do is nothing new. After Wayne finished beating all of us three or four games, Doc had had enough.

"You know we don't have to just sit here, bored. Wayne, tell these guys what we did last week," Doc said.

"Nah, they wouldn't want to hear about it. It's not their kind of fun," he said.

Of course Ronny and I looked at them in disbelief. We did everything together, and if someone was missing, you heard about it the next day. So the idea that they did something that no one else in our group knew about? That didn't add up.

"Okay, I'll tell them," Doc said.

"No!" shouted Wayne. "We swore it to secrecy, to Eddie, we wouldn't tell anyone."

"Who the frig is Eddie?" Ronny asked. "And why wouldn't you tell us? We're your best friends since elementary school."

"Ugghhh," grunted Wayne. "Eddie is from shop class and he said he would break our faces if we told anyone."

"You mean Eddie Sparinger? That guy can barely talk," I said. "Why would you hang out with him and then not tell us?"

"Eddie's not too bright, I'll give you that," Doc said, "but he is hilarious, in his own way. So we were grinding a piece of metal in class, and it flew off the grinder and nearly killed our teacher and Eddie started laughing and, well, I don't know, he just started talking to us about his interesting hobbies."

"Interesting hobbies?" I asked.

"Like what, torturing animals? Pushing people down stairs? Stealing kids' lunch money?" Ronny added.

"No, not like that…well at least not when we are around," Wayne said.

"Real nice," Ronny said, slowly and sarcastically. "Is that why you said you were busy last Thursday when I tried to get you to go with me to the mall?"

"Yes, but I'm telling you this kid is not that bad. Well, he is, but he's kind of fun. So, remember that kid who always picked on me in 5th grade? Jaime Wessler? So Eddie, and this is the great part, he says to us do we want to have some fun and do we have someone who needs payback? So I think of him and so we drive by his house real slow and we …" Wayne looked at Doc for approval.

"Go ahead now. You already told them everything anyway."

"So we drive by real slow and we start egging his house. Like two dozen eggs. And the best part is he comes out and I pop him right in the head. It was hilarious. Like Halloween but way better because it wasn't. You know what I mean?"

Ronny and I just stared in disbelief.

"Soooo, what do you guys think? Hilarious right?" Wayne asked.

"C'mon guys, it's pretty funny. Believe me, you'd love it if you came out with us," Doc said.

"I'm in," Ronny said. "Let's go egging. That's awesome. Who knew you could egg things when it wasn't Halloween?"

Now, in hindsight, I was usually a little more sensible, even as a teenager, and definitely more cautious about committing acts of mischief. But teenage boys have hormones and sometimes it's tough to say why they do what they do. Plus, they were all looking at me, waiting for my approval, because apparently it was needed to proceed.

"All right. Let's do it," I said.

We hit the corner store and loaded up on eight dozen eggs. The guy at the counter didn't even blink, just took our cash and said have a good night. Then we rolled out. Each of us had to come up with one target, which wasn't hard to do.

I won't lie, it was rather empowering to just drive by and hurl eggs at people you could never stand. There is also the excitement that comes with the thought of getting spotted and recognized or of getting caught. But we knew we would never get caught. It was a victimless crime, just wacky teenage fun. Sure, that one kid was screaming, "I've been hit!" over and over while his little brother screamed, "Johnny stay down! They're everywhere!" but in the rush of the moment it seemed harmless enough.

"We still have four dozen eggs," Doc said. "Time for round two."

"What's round two?" I asked.

"Well, Eddie showed us this spot that's got real good cover to hide, over on Henderson. It's a big wooded lot, a few acres deep, that's for sale. We hid out there and nailed cars the other night," Wayne said.

This was a different matter. It didn't seem like a good idea. It seemed like a good way to get caught. You weren't able to get away as fast and even though we had been egging the jerks from our past, these were just random people who didn't deserve our wrath and retribution.

"I don't know about that," I started to say, when Doc cut me off.

"C'mon, man. It's the same thing. I'll drop you guys off, park a ways away, and we will unleash these eggs on cars as they whiz by. It's harder than it looks. The cars are moving and they never stop. It's challenging and fun. Besides, the lot is huge and runs all the way back to that development, so we can always run out the back if we need to."

They all started in again, assuring me it was going to be great, more difficult than egging a house, more fun than I thought. So, for the second time that night, I agreed.

Doc pulled up and we jumped out quick, carrying our eggs carefully so as to not break a single one. He sped off and parked somewhere a long ways off, because it was more than 20 minutes of hiding in the brush waiting for him to show up.

When he arrived, we settled into a spot behind some trees, looking down at Henderson Street just a few feet below us. Cars were whizzing past. The speed limit was only 40 mph but no one was going that slow. It was going to take great timing to hit a car dead on.

"Okay, here's what we do," Wayne explained, "we watch for a car, count three, and all fire. We're bound to hit it."

Your heart starts to race a little as the anticipation builds. Doc picked out a white sedan up the road. "That white one coming, ready, one, two, three!"

We all fired. My shot went high over the roof. Ronny missed and so did Wayne. Doc managed to hit the rear bumper. There was no way the driver even heard it. "See, I told you it was hard!"

We tried again and again, with me missing shot after shot. I was genuinely frustrated. I was a good shot with a good throwing arm. I couldn't believe I could miss that many times. Then the teasing started. "Man, you stink!" Ronny said. "Maybe we should ask them to slow down for you," Doc laughed. "My sister throws better than you," Wayne added. That was it. Now I was determined.

"Next car, I'm hitting dead on," I said.

A big SUV was coming fast. "That one," I said as I pointed, "on three!"

We unleashed our eggs over Henderson in a hail. One, two, three, four direct hits. Victory! I smiled as I saw my egg slide down the driver's side window, saw the driver's look of shock. And then we heard as he locked up his brakes and watched as he whipped over to the shoulder of the road. One, two, three, four, five, six, big men jumped out of the maroon SUV. The driver was in a rage, screaming, cussing, while his buddies pointed to the woods behind them.

They all bolted across the road toward us. We looked at each other in panic and disbelief. Then we dropped our eggs and ran. The lot was overgrown and full of dead underbrush and pricker bushes. Something like a trail was winding through the mess, but we scattered. All I could think of was the end of *Lord of the Flies* when Ralph runs through the jungle like an animal. It was dark and I tripped on a root or a log and went flat on my face. Just then, behind me, I heard voices coming. I could see several people coming up the trail. I rolled over behind a tree and stayed still. They were moving at a fast trot, but not running the way I had. I could only see their shapes it was so dark. I waited for thirty seconds and was about to get out of there, when I heard much angrier voices coming. I immediately knew my mistake. The first group was my friends. I forgot how slow they were. The second group was larger, some of them carrying sticks, and talking, or more like screaming, they were going to kill us when they found us.

It was a surreal moment. How did I get here? Why would I ever do this? And yet, here I was, crouched down in the woods, wishing I hadn't worn shorts, scratched and bleeding, hoping no one saw me. They moved past me in the dark, not seeing me just twenty feet away, and I started hoping my friends had picked up the pace before these guys caught them. I could hear my own breathing, it seemed so loud, and I tried to figure out my next move. If they caught up to Wayne, Ronny, and Doc, they were dead. Then I heard them turning around, cursing us, giving up the chase and heading back towards the road. I wished I had not tripped; if I had just kept running we'd all have been in the clear.

I watched, frozen, as they filed past me. Their voices were louder, even angrier, now that we had escaped them. The one out front was the one driving. He was seething, spitting and making sounds, more than words or sentences. I didn't even want to breathe. As they walked past, I could feel my escape coming. I would sit still for a few minutes to make sure they were gone, then move as quietly as I could towards where I had last seen my friends headed.

One by one they passed, all six of them, heading toward their vehicle. I was shaking from the adrenaline rush and about to breathe out when the last one turned and stared in my direction.

"Hey," he said, his friends ignoring him. "Is that, is it, a person? By that tree?"

Just enough of me was sticking out that even in the dark it looked like something. I stayed perfectly still. Again, in hindsight, I probably should have bolted. I still wonder if I could have outrun them all. But I didn't. I just stayed still.

"No, I think it is," the last man said. "Guys, get back here! That's one over there!"

They surrounded me in an instant. It was like a scene from the Museum of Natural History. Six big grunting men, wielding clubs, with me at the center of the circle, prey. I held up my hands and tried to be calm. "Okay, you got me," I said.

"I am going to kill you!" the driver said to me. "Do you know what you did to my ride?"

Fortunately for me, two of his friends grabbed him. "Easy, man, the cops were already called. Let's just give him to them."

They marched me out of the woods in front of them, their trophy, with the driver cussing me out and threatening me the whole way. The police officer, the intense one who vehemently berated me and who informed me how lucky I was that I was one block out of his jurisdiction, was waiting on the side of the road. My heart sank. I never felt so stupid in my whole life. I was doing the most ridiculously juvenile thing I could and now I was busted. My parents were going to kill me.

Officer Finley arrived just as Officer Super Intense was reaching his crescendo, and rescued me by putting me in the back of his squad car. I didn't have any I.D. on me, so he asked me for my info and then ran it. "Well, kid, the good news is you're clean, if you are who you say you are, and I think you are. First time offender, huh? Give me a minute to go talk to these guys."

He got out and left me alone. I was praying so hard to make it out of this situation. I was terrified of calling home to get bailed out of jail. How do you explain to your father that you went down the street to play ping-pong at your friend's house and ended up in jail in the next town over? The conversation outside the car was heated, but I couldn't hear anything. The driver of the car was throwing his hands up and down, pointing at me and then at his SUV. After a couple of minutes, the other officer left, and the college kids got back into their truck. Officer Finley got back in the car with me.

"Okay, kid, here's the deal. This guy can press charges against you, but he might be persuaded to settle for damages, if there are any, after he washes his car and checks it out. Eggs can damage the paint. Did you know that? You'll be in the police blotter, but considering the situation, that's not so bad, really. You could have killed someone. Imagine an old woman driving down this road and she gets hit in the windshield and swerves off the road. Would you want that to happen to your grandmother?"

"No sir. It was stupid. I don't know why I did it. I just, I just…didn't think." I could hear my Dad's voice then, telling me to do just that. I sounded remorseful, because I was, and must have looked pathetic, scratched and bloodied.

"I believe you are," he said. He gave me a pretty good lecture about growing up and not being stupid, and when he finished, he added, "Just one more thing. This guy wants the names of your friends so they are on the hook, too. I'll call their parents and let them know the situation."

I stared at him in shock. I couldn't give up my friends. It just wasn't done. Think of all the expressions: Better dead than red. Snitches get stitches, or end up in ditches. Death before dishonor. Rats get poisoned. I don't know, there was a lot going through my head. I looked at him, and then down at the floor, and said, "I was by myself. There wasn't anyone with me."

He let out a chortle and a snort, then a good laugh. "Come on kid, you mean to tell me you came out here by yourself to egg cars?"

"Yes, sir."

"Seriously, just tell me who they are and you can all share the punishment."

"It was just me."

He stared at me hard and his little smile disappeared. "Kid, you really want to do this? He might want to press charges if he doesn't get the names."

"There are no names. It's just me."

"Hmm. Okay, you want to play it that way. I understand loyalty, but this might go bad." He got out of the car, but didn't close the door all the way. He approached the SUV and I could hear them talking.

"Are you kidding me?" the driver shouted. "There's no way he was alone!"

"Calm down, sir. What do you want to do? I can give you his info and you settle it yourself, or we can all go to the station and do the paperwork. Your choice, but I can tell you the kid's clean, and he's scared to death."

The driver looked at his watch. Then his friends started in. "We're already late, man. Just take the info and let's go. It's not worth wrecking the whole night over some stupid kids." The driver reached out, took the paper with my info from the policeman, and took off.

Officer Finley climbed back into the car. "So, here's how this works. Like I said, I have to put something in the blotter. That guy has your info. Expect a call tomorrow if he sees any damage to his vehicle. You get to pay it. This whole thing is on you now."

"I understand."

He shook his head. "Kids never stop surprising you," he said. "Do you need a ride home?"

"No," I said. "My cousin lives around the corner. I'll get a ride from my aunt."

"All right," he said, "and remember what I said. It's time to grow up. No more stupid stuff like this."

He let me out of the back of the car and I started walking towards where my imaginary aunt lived. There was no way I was getting dropped off by a squad car. Officer Finley drove away. I was in disbelief. I wondered what happened to my friends, but I had a long walk to think about it. Five minutes later, a car pulled up behind me on the side of the road. My heart dropped as I thought those college kids had come back for me, but it was no mistaking Doc's '83 Chevy Chevette.

They jumped out and grabbed me. "Dude, what happened? We drove by and saw the cops and kept going!

How did you get out? We thought you were going to be calling for bail!"

"So did I," I said. "But I'll tell you the story starting from when you friggin' asthmatics came by me in the woods until I told the cops I am the world's biggest loser egging cars alone on a Wednesday night. You idiots better be prepared to help me pay for damages too, if I get the call."

They all stared at me until Wayne started laughing. "Well, at least it will make a great story to tell Eddie tomorrow."

"Screw Eddie," I said. "This is what you get when you listen to Eddie's advice on how to have fun? I'll stick to doing it my way, thanks."

"What are you so pissed about?" Doc asked, but I ignored him and got in the backseat.

ASYLUM

The alarm clock went off at 6:30a.m., but I was already awake. I woke up five minutes earlier and tried to go back for that extra five minutes, but I'd dose off just long enough to wake up and see the minute change. The alarm was loud, most mornings I wouldn't budge, and I didn't want to wake my parents, so at exactly 6:30 I hit the off button.

Hurrying into the bathroom, careful to shut the door gently, I started splashing cold water on my face as the events from last night played over in my head. It all seemed dreamlike. Around midnight I had slipped out quietly and met my friend and his older brother at the vacant lot. We made a quick transfer from their trunk to mine and then I was home in bed again, waiting for the alarm to go off.

I put on the same pair of jeans I wore the day before. It takes a couple of days to get them broken in just right. Then I slipped out to my car before my parents woke up and checked my trunk. I snuck a quick peek to make sure the goods were still there and then shut it. Three cases of beer, safe and sound. I had never done anything quite like this before, even though I had pulled some ridiculous stunts. The idea of leaving my friends behind to start college next fall was beginning to seem more and more real, and we all wanted to have one more adventure to remember our final days of high school. After all, what else would we talk about in twenty years at the reunion?

We were all meeting at McDonald's at seven, but I knew everyone would be late. The quicker I got away from the house the better, I thought. That gave me less of a chance for something to go wrong. Plus, I was hungry, so I decided I'd eat and wait for them to show.

Ronny came in first, dragging Jason with him to the booth where I was sitting. Jason was rubbing his eyes and yawning with his mouth wide open. Ronny's dark eyes flashed and I could tell he had just finished yelling at Jason for something. "It's twenty after seven," I said. "Where you guys been?"

"Ask Sleeping Beauty over here," Ronny said, pointing his thumb at Jason. "I couldn't get him out of bed. His mommy had to wake him up."

"Hey, you want to shut up already, Ronald?" Jason said. "I need my beauty sleep!"

"It's not helping," I said and Ronny laughed. He stretched and ran his fingers through his hair and yawned, then dug into his jeans for some money.

"I'm starving, Jason. Let's grab something to eat before we go."

The two of them went up to order breakfast while I sat and finished my hotcakes and sausage. I watched Jason, always so laid back, tug at Ronny's t-shirt to tease him a little now that he was calmed down. My stomach was a knot, partly because I knew how much fun today would be, and partly because I was afraid someone was going to find out what I had in the trunk of my car. I thought about going to check it one more time when my other two friends I was waiting for came in. Wayne and Doc, dressed like the rest of us in t-shirts and jeans, both wearing ball caps and new Nikes, walked right past me to get something to eat.

Ronny and Jason sat down and Wayne and Doc

followed. "I can't believe you asked for ketchup," Wayne was saying. "That's disgusting."

"I like it like that," Doc said as he smothered his Egg McMuffin.

I rolled my eyes and thought, "Here we go again." Wayne and Doc would fight over absolutely anything. This time, Wayne was clearly disgusted by the use of ketchup and didn't care who in the restaurant knew it. Wayne was a big guy, but Doc was bigger at 6' 2". He was used to Wayne's ranting because they had been best friends since they were five. So, Doc did what he always did – he ignored Wayne, did things his way, and ate his breakfast.

"Hey, what time is it, Wayne?" I asked, trying to get his attention and keep him from going off again.

"Quarter to eight," he said. "Shouldn't we get going?"

"It's kind of early to start drinking though," Ronny said. "We have lots of time."

"The sooner the better," Wayne said. "I wanna get ripped today!"

"There's no problem with that," I said. "My trunk is filled up and ready to go."

"You've already got all the beer in your trunk?" Jason asked. "When'd you do that?"

"Last night," Doc answered. "Me and my brother met him and put it all in so we'd be ready today. And that reminds me Jason, you still owe me for the brew, so pay up."

We had decided weeks ago that we'd ditch school and spend one last day doing nothing. The only real problem was not everyone could get away with missing school. It was risky. It wasn't just your parents that you worried about. The school tried to keep seniors from skipping at the end of the year and called home. It took a lot of preparation to take a day off. Not everyone could do it.

Ronny's parents had a cabin at a lake, so we decided we'd go north for the day since it was only an hour away. All of us climbed into my car, which was a tight squeeze for the guys in the back. It was a two door 1970 Chevy Malibu, with a 350 engine and a floor column gearshift. It was not perfect, more of a work in progress, but for a first car it was awesome. The sun was out, it was already 75 degrees, the windows were down and the radio was cranked up. We were laughing and not paying attention to the radio when they said something about our high school.

"Hey, what did they just say?" Doc asked.

"It was something about school," I said, "but I'm not sure what."

"I've got an idea," Wayne said. "Let's go by the school."

"Are you crazy?" I said. "My trunk is full of beer and we're all cutting classes and you want to go by the school?"

"Yeah, but don't you get it?" he asked.

"Get what? It's the dumbest thing I ever heard."

"Wait, I know what he's saying," Jason jumped in. "There's supposed to be a big thing where all the juniors walk out today. We could pick up some fleeing junior girls when they come out and take them with us."

"No way. We planned this skip day for a month and that's suicide," I said. "Besides, why are the juniors walking out anyway?"

"You didn't hear?" Doc asked. "Some kid got the measles so they canceled the Junior Prom tomorrow. Yesterday, a bunch of juniors started passing out flyers to walk out and protest it. It should be pretty wild…if they go through with it."

"C'mon, let's go see what happens. It'll only take a minute," Jason said.

"Nothing'll happen," Ronny pleaded.

"We won't get caught," Doc begged.

"Let's check it out," Wayne whined.

A car full of your friends ganging up on you is a lot of peer pressure. I caved in.

"All right, we'll go. But we're not going on school grounds. We'll watch from across the street, okay?"

Everyone agreed this was a brilliant plan, since technically we wouldn't be on school grounds to get caught for anything. It sounded good to me, too. It was kind of an adventure, which is what we were looking for, and at the same time it felt safe, because it was only our school we were going to see. It wasn't much different than going to a basketball game. The more we talked, the better the idea got. It was a great way to start our day. Maybe we would pick up a few girls. What could possibly go wrong?

"Oh my God! Is that News Channel 2?" Ronny yelled.

"It is Channel 2!" Jason shouted. "What are they doing here?"

I pulled the car over, maybe fifty feet from the news van, and tried to suppress the surrealism I was experiencing. I should have kept driving.

"Holy crap! There's a news crew here!" I screamed. "What is going on?"

I stared into the backseat at the blank faces staring back.

If only one of them had yelled "Drive!" we would have been long gone. Instead, we were paralyzed with wonder. Tap, tap, tap. Tap, tap, tap. I turned around to see a reporter peering in at me. She snuck up on my blind side and brought a cameraman.

"Are you part of the protest? Do you go to school here? Are any of you juniors? Who wants to do an interview? Joe, are you getting a shot of this?"

Joe, the cameraman, was directly in front of my car, starting to film us. As he moved around to get a good look in the windows, we started yelling at him. "No cameras! No cameras!"

"Joe, shut that camera off," she told him. Then, turning back to us, "Wouldn't one of you like to do an interview with me?"

"Let's go guys, we'll be famous!" Wayne shouted as he opened the door, pushed my seat forward and hopped out of the car. "My name's Wayne," he started saying. "How did Channel 2 know about this anyway?"

"Joe, get that camera over here for an interview, NOW!" We didn't know the news was told to stay off campus. They were desperate for a story since they came here for something. But this reporter was cool. She knew how to get the story. She told Wayne that some students had called in and told their side of the story. She just wanted to get the facts straight. Wayne was the perfect student. He just needed to look at her and answer her questions. Then Joe started filming.

"So, you are skipping school today as a way to cause a riot?" she asked.

"No, what?" Wayne was immediately confused. The questions came, rapid fire, and all she needed was a snippet of him confessing to something, anything, to have a scoop. Wayne didn't do well. He was more of a gym and lunch guy than a debate and public speaking guy.

"Why are you trying to disrupt the school system? Are you against education?"

"Huh? I'm still not following..."

"Are you the mastermind behind this plot to walk out? Why are you parked over here? Why did you skip school? Are you picking people up? Who are your friends? Do you skip school a lot? What do you hope to accomplish with this plan?"

"I just...wanted breakfast. Once I skipped school to get a haircut." He sounded like an idiot. It would have been hilarious to watch if we weren't all afraid we were dead. There was no way to avoid getting caught. The only question was should I drive away and leave him.

None of us wanted to get out of the car and get him. The camera was out there. The fewer pictures of us the better. So, instead, we watched the next five minutes from the relative safety of the car as Wayne was grilled and forced to confess to things he never did. Finally, we couldn't take it.

"You go get him," I said to Doc. "Just drag him back in here."

"No way," Doc said. "If you want him, you get him."

Jason and Ronny stayed completely silent, keeping their heads down. In the rear view mirror I noticed a car pull up behind us. I turned to see a group of juniors I recognized getting out.

"Uh oh. That's them," Ronny said. "All of them got suspended yesterday for passing out those flyers."

"They really got suspended for that?"

"Yeah. Mr. Corpsen called it an attempt to start a riot and disrupt the educational system."

"Wow. How long are they out for?"

"I heard five days, but maybe more."

This was our chance to free Wayne, so I yelled out my window. "Hey," I said to the reporter, "those are the juniors who set everything up. You should talk to them!"

The camera turned to catch them getting out of their car, and the reporter, forgetting Wayne, went to them. Doc reached out the window, grabbed Wayne, and pulled him towards the car telling him to "GET IN!" At the same moment a flood of students came out from the school, followed by Mr. Corpsen with a bullhorn ordering the students to turn around and go back to class. He was largely ignored. Still, he persisted.

"We know who you are and you will be written up. Do not leave the school grounds. Return to class. Return to class!"

Students were chanting and running. The juniors behind us were screaming and jumping up and down, waving and shouting at the students across the street to join them, and the News Channel 2 team was having a field day. I threw the car into gear and tore up the road, squealing tires and blowing exhaust smoke everywhere. Everyone turned to Wayne.

"What? I thought we were all getting out?" Wayne said.

"You idiot!"

"How could one guy be so stupid!"

"Where is your brain?"

"But I thought…I thought we were all getting out?"

"Well what do we do now?" Ronny asked. "If my parents see that, I'm dead."

"Maybe we should just forget the whole thing," Jason said. "Just head home and lay low."

"Are you all crazy?" Doc asked. "We are not quitting now. We have the whole day. The stupid news isn't on until six. Besides, do you think they'll show footage of Wayne when they have the entire walk out on camera? And they were interviewing the juniors who were suspended – they started the whole thing. They only have about two minutes for this whole story when they put it on T.V. and we were the least important thing that happened. We will not be put on the air; no one will ever see us."

"He's right," I said. "I say we go with the plan. Who's in?"

"Okay, I'm in," Jason said.

"Me too," Ronny added. "No one will ever know. I panicked a little."

"But, I thought we were all getting out or I never would have gone," Wayne said.

"Then it's unanimous," Doc declared. "Head north."

Free and easy at last, we drove north until houses spread out and fields came into view. It was a beautiful day for skipping school and drinking beer. We felt like the worst was behind and we could just enjoy our last "school outing." We turned the music up again and started making jokes about how brilliant Wayne's interview was. He didn't think it was that funny.

"Hey, look over there," Wayne said. "There's a couple of deer in that field."

We all turned to look. What I didn't see was the deer crossing the road in front of me. I turned my head back and screamed, swerved to the right, off the road and onto the gravel shoulder narrowly missing the deer. As I tried to get control and back onto the road, there was a boom and then more swerving as I got control and came to a stop. My heart was racing. I told myself to breathe as I got out to check the damage. The guys in the backseat were white as sheets. Doc was gripping the dashboard, white knuckled.

"Ahhh…this isn't good," I said as I looked at the damage. "The tire's blown out and…the muffler is hanging."

The guys got out. "Do you have a spare and a jack?" Wayne asked.

"Yeah, it's in the trunk." We set the beer in the weeds by the side of the road, out of sight. Then Wayne started jacking up the car. Doc tied up the muffler. It was loud, but okay to get home. My spare tire was not good. It had been someone's regular tire at one time. It was kind of bald and generally well used. We did a good job getting the car together, but now it was pushing noon. I didn't want to say what I was thinking.

"I think we have to head back," I finally said. "This tire is pretty bad and I'll get a ticket for the muffler if I get pulled over."

"Oh man. This sucks," Wayne said.

"I know. But I have a plan. We'll head back and check in at home. Then we'll go out and do something tonight. Hey, it's Friday night, we have all this beer, and we're good to go."

This was not what anyone really wanted, but it was what it was – a bad situation. Everyone agreed at least we had tonight to party. "Hey, get the beer and put it in the trunk," I said to Doc.

He jumped in next to me and said, "I think there's a cop coming up the road. You better take off!" No one wanted to get caught with a trunk full of beer so we were gone.

When we got home, we stopped at Wayne's to transfer the beer. My car was going to be out of commission for a couple days until it was fixed. He opened the back of his ride, a 1986 Ford Bronco II, and I popped my trunk.

"Doc," I said, "how many cases of beer did you put in my trunk?"

"Both of them," he said.

"Both? There were three. You left a whole case of beer in the ditch!"

"What? I wouldn't..."

"But you did. Come on, man. That's going to cost you."

Wayne came by to pick me up early, so I could be out before my parents came in. I left them a note that I'd be back by curfew. We went over to Jason's basement to hang out while we waited for the other guys. The news came on. About twenty minutes in they said the story about our school was next. When it aired, the first shot had my car in the background. Then it cut to a couple of interviews with the juniors who lead the rebellion, then to a shot of kids fleeing the school. It was mayhem. I kind of wished we had stayed to watch more of it. Just when we thought the piece was over, they cut to Wayne's interview.

"Why did you skip school today? What statement do you

want to make?" the reporter asked. She wasn't on camera, just Wayne's face, and I was pretty sure her questions were a voice over.

"I skipped school to get a haircut," Wayne said. He looked like a complete idiot.

The reporter said, "There you have it, Tom. Some students wanted to make a point, some just wanted a haircut. Back to you."

The anchor man, Tom, was laughing. "Well, we all want something," he said and went to commercial. We looked at Wayne and died laughing.

"You're going to be the haircut kid forever," Jason said.

"Shut up! That's not even what I said!"

Ten minutes later the other guys busted in and let Wayne have it. He was tortured with that story for the next ten years and it still comes up sometimes. "Let's just get going," Wayne finally said.

"What's the plan for tonight?" Doc asked.

"I'm starving. Let's get pizza first and figure it out," Ronny answered.

As we sat eating slices in the pizzeria, we ran into some more guys from school. "What are you boys up to tonight?" I asked.

"Not much," Dave answered. "It's pretty dead tonight. We were talking about going up to the abandoned insane asylum to check it out. You interested?"

The asylum had been in the news about a month before. It was closed down about twenty years ago and was considered off limits. At least, that's what we thought until the police raided it on a tip and found that the basement was being used for some cult worship. For about three or four months before the raid, a lot of pets had started going missing. It turned out this cult was sacrificing animals, worshiping the devil, doing occult rituals – the whole deal. The night they busted it no one was there, so they just confiscated everything and locked the place up tighter. The news the next day showed pictures from the police. There was an altar and a bunch of burned up bones. They had an upside down cross and pentagrams all over and a lot of candles. It was kind of a cliché satanic cult if you want to know the truth, but it was still super creepy. Of course we wanted to go see it.

I looked at my friends who were all nodding. "Yeah, we're in," I said. "We just need to make one stop first. We'll meet you at the convenience store up the road in a few minutes."

"No problem. We were going to tell a few more people. We'll meet you there." Then, turning to Wayne he joked, "By the way, nice haircut."

We had to stop at the convenience store for ice. We'd driven our beer around all day. It was time to drink some but it was warm. "Where's the cooler?" I asked, looking under the blanket in the back of Wayne's Bronco.

"Doc, did you grab the cooler out of my garage like I told you?" Wayne asked.

"I told Ronny to get it," Doc replied.

"I told Jason to get it," Ronny jumped in.

"I told Doc to get it himself," Jason said.

"Well that's just great. We waited all day and no one can do one thing right. Come on guys. This is bush league."

"Just open the cases and ice them down," Doc said. "It'll be fine."

"Fine until it melts all over my truck," Wayne said.

"It's this or warm beer. What do you want?" Doc shot back. Then he iced the beer.

On the way to the asylum we started to realize we had a lot of cars following us. Dave had told someone, and they told someone else, and pretty soon we were a convoy fifteen cars deep. As we pulled up to the asylum it was just getting dark. It was definitely scarier in person than on the news or in the paper. Suddenly, no one wanted to go inside. We all got out, it had to be sixty teenagers or more, and stared up at this gothic insane asylum.

"Who's going in?" Dave asked. There were no volunteers.

Doc opened the back of the Bronco and popped the first beer of the night. It was the start of a party. Everyone that had beer decided it was a good time and place to drink it. Everyone that didn't tried to mooch one off the rest of us. "Well, I think I'll stay here and watch the beer," Doc said. "It's not cold yet and I don't want any of these moochers stealing it."

"I'm staying to watch Doc, so he doesn't drink it all," Wayne said.

"Me too," Jason put in.

In all honesty, I wasn't crazy about the idea of breaking into this building either. First, I was sure we were trespassing. Second, this place was as eerie as it gets.

"What's a matter, you guys afraid of ghosts?" Dave chided us. Only all of the kids who came with him weren't volunteering to go in either. In fact, most of the people there were just happy to have a place to hang out with other kids. Doc, gesturing with his beer, was already talking to a couple of girls who followed us here. I was thinking he had the right idea.

"Well, I didn't come here for nothing," Dave said. "I'm going in. Who's with me?"

All of those kids and not one volunteer. I couldn't take it, so I said, "I'm in, Dave. Let's go."

"Me too," Ronny said, surprising us both.

"All right. It's the three of us," Dave said, now smiling. "We'll have a story to tell these wusses when we're done!"

We went around the back of the asylum and found a point of entry. The police had nailed boards over all of the lower windows and doors but not the ones higher up. By giving Dave a boost, he could get on a small porch roof over an exit door and then in a broken window. I pushed Ronny up behind Dave and then they both hoisted me up. We were in.

Inside it was everything we imagined. It was mostly deserted, but there were still a few items: iron bed frames with wrist straps, old empty bottles for pills, bedpans, and a pile of dirty sheets. There was also a variety of leaves and small branches and it was obvious birds and other animals had come through the open window. It smelled of earth and decay and animal feces tinged, just faintly, with institutional disinfectant. It was ghostly the way the shadows danced in the room with the moonlight.

"This place gives me the chills," Ronny said.

In the corner, the pile of bed sheets started to move. "That's it, I'm gone," Dave said as he headed for the window.

"Dave, wait..." I said, but he didn't. He jumped from the porch roof and ran for the cars. I crept closer to the moving pile until I saw a tail. "Is that...is that a rat?"

It poked its head out and looked at us, confused to see us no doubt. "It's a raccoon!" Ronny said, relieved it wasn't something worse.

"Better leave it alone, it could have rabies."

"I wasn't going to pet it."

We walked out into the hallway. There were a lot of strange sounds coming from the rooms, in the ceiling, below us. We startled some pigeons which flew by and I almost peed myself. "Okay, Ron, we've been inside. This place gives me the creeps. I say we follow Dave out of here."

"Good idea, but..."

"But what?"

"We've come this far. Want to take a look at the basement?"

"Are you nuts?" I asked, and I meant it.

"This is the place for it," Ronny joked. "Besides, you know Stacy Williams? I kind of told her I wasn't coming back until I saw where they did all the animal sacrifices in the devil worshipping temple."

"Why would you tell her that?"

"Duh! To impress her because I like her. Plus she said if I did that she'd go with me to the Senior Prom."

"Ron, you already have a date to the prom."

"Yeah, but I don't like her. Stacy has better...assets. And she's prettier."

"Look, if she says she'll go because you pull this stunt, it's probably because she already likes you and would go anyways. So let's just go and tell her we saw it. Who's going to doubt us? It's just you and me."

"No. I have to do it for real. She'll know."

"Jeeeeeeeeeez. Okay. Let's go quick."

We walked down the hall until we found a staircase to the first floor. It was worse than the second floor, leaving me to believe we were descending straight into hell. After ten minutes of looking, we still couldn't find the entrance to the basement. This place was big, not to mention dark. We opened one door and it was a room with a gurney and what looked like an electric chair.

"What is that?" Ronny asked. "Did they kill people here? Give 'em the chair?"

"I don't think so. I think it was used for shock therapy. It's supposed to be awful."

Then we heard a noise. It sounded like someone dropped a safe down a flight of stairs, only it was in the room next to us. We freaked. "Let's go," I said.

"Yep."

We headed back towards the stairs to the second floor and I saw an open door. It was the staircase to the basement. We stopped and looked down into the darkness. Something was moving down there, we could hear it. A shadow went by the bottom of the steps.

"Did you see that?" Ronny whispered.

I didn't answer. I just ran up the stairs. Ronny was right behind me. We found the room we came into. The raccoon was nowhere to be seen. Through the open window we heard a new sound – sirens.

"Uh oh," I said. "That can't be good."

We jumped out the window onto the roof and hurried down. We could hear cars starting up and driving off. I could hear Wayne and Doc calling us, yelling to hurry as they saw us running. Somehow, the Bronco was full of people. Cars were driving off in all directions. Kids were just jumping in any available ride. It was a melee of people fighting to get a ride with anyone, just to get out of there. Wayne spun around and drove towards us.

"Just jump in the back!" he said. As he pulled ahead of us we dove, face first into the back of the truck. Someone reached back and grabbed us. Ronny started to slide out as Wayne cornered hard. He kicked at the blanket, knocking it and two cases of beer out and onto the ground, the sound of breaking bottles and spinning gravel mixed with screams and shouts and sirens. I managed to reach and grab the hatch, slamming it down and screaming, "Go, go, go!" as Wayne drove like a wild man onto the pavement and off into the night.

A mile down the road, when we realized we weren't being followed, I took a good look at who we had picked up. Counting Ronny and I, there were ten of us, six in the backseat alone. Doc had some girl I didn't recognize on his lap in the front. Ronny looked up to see who had pulled him in and was still hanging on to his hand. It was Stacy. Ronny smiled at her. "Wait until I tell you what we saw in there…"

"Hey," Doc interrupted him, "pass us up a couple of beers."

"Remember this morning," I asked Doc, "when you left that beer?"

"Yeah.

"We're even."

When I finally got home that night it felt like the longest day of my life. It was by far the craziest. I had wanted one last adventure with my friends. In a way, we had it, minus the beer. I walked into the kitchen to grab a sandwich and some milk. I was surprised to see my dad come in, but I shouldn't have been.

"Hey. You missed curfew."

"Sorry dad. I tried to get home, but Wayne was driving."

"I saw your car. What happened?"

"I blew out a tire and wrecked my muffler. Can you help me fix it tomorrow?"

"Sure. And I won't tell mom you came in late. You boys weren't out drinking or anything, right?"

"Nope." I could honestly say I wasn't.

"End of your senior year. I just want you to stay out of trouble."

"I'm trying, dad."

"Good. Oh and son…"

"Yeah dad?"

"When you see Wayne tomorrow, tell him I said nice haircut."

ACKNOWLEDGEMENTS

I would like to acknowledge all those who helped me become the writer I am today. Diane Matza, who started me off when she told me I was good at this, Eugene Nassar and Frank Bergmann, who taught me to love literature I didn't know existed, Mary Anne Hutchinson and Mary Ann Janda, who let me run free, John Cormican, who taught me that language is words but more than words, and Jerry Cartwright, who spent countless hours teaching me to be a creative writer, I thank you all. A special thank you also goes to Martha Tuck Rozett, who reignited my passion for writing while driving home revision, revision, revision. It worked.

I would also like to acknowledge all of my friends and family who I trusted with my stories. Sean, Chas, Rebecca, Alyssa, and Kelly, thank you. Your input was invaluable. Kristine, Maddy, and Sam, thanks for believing. I love you all.

Finally, Anne Lamott, your book *Bird by Bird* is amazing. It should be required in every creative writing class. Thank you. Let's do lunch sometime. My treat.

ABOUT THE AUTHOR

Andrew Puckey is an English teacher and adjunct professor of literature and writing in Central New York. He currently teaches at Whitesboro High School, where he has been working for more than a decade. When not teaching, he enjoys spending time in the Adirondacks with his wife and two children, and their dogs Jake and Ginger.